LEAVING
GEORGE

A gripping thriller, full of suspense

DIANE M DICKSON

THE
BOOK
FOLKS

Paperback published by The Book Folks

London, 2018

© Diane Dickson

ISBN 978-1-7200-9341-1

www.thebookfolks.com

For my family.

Chapter 1

She'd done it – she'd left him.

She would miss the cat.

The front door slammed as Pauline stepped into the bright day full of sunshine and hope. Her face lifted in a smile. She hardly dared to believe that at last it might all be behind her; the lies, the fear and the fraudulent image that life had become.

As she took the first steps her insides bubbled with a breathless excitement. The thrill was tenuous though; a traitorous worry squirmed beneath the pleasure. She tried to ignore it but the sliver of fear had her glancing at her watch. Even as her feet covered the ground, her brain played and re-played the plan and the timings, the what-ifs and maybes.

The little pink phone had blinked from the hall stand as she'd passed. There had been a moment's hesitation but she could take no risk that he might trace her. She had read that the police, if he went to them, could find the location of a mobile if it was switched on and so she had left it behind.

Perhaps it had been him calling? He had received no answer. What would he do? Maybe she should have answered.

It could have been him and now she had missed the chance to reassure him that all was as normal.

Should she go back?

Perhaps she should go back, call him. She could pretend to be checking the time he was due home.

But a deeper part of herself knew it was too late to go back now.

She mustn't go back, must never go back. She paused, took a steadying breath. It was essential to remain calm, to be strong.

Her beautiful garden glowed in the late morning heat and she filled her eyes with a last lingering look and tucked the memory away. Haze was already rising from the road surface so she squeezed her jacket into the top of the bag, dragged off her knitted hat and pushed a hand through her short brown hair. She had a long walk ahead and although she knew the timings from driving the route, the estimate she had made for the journey on foot was little more a calculated guess. Then her gaze was pulled to the car port and she frowned sadly at the little blue Peugeot snoozing in the shade. It would be so much easier to slide into the plastic scented heat and drive away in comfort.

Yet like the phone, taking the car would only increase the chances that George might find her and so it must be forfeit.

This plan had been forming for years, ever since the first blows, the early bruises. It had begun as a wish, grown into hope and now it was the only way: it was essential that she escape.

As her husband of twenty years snored on the settee, she had schemed and calculated. She would leave him, when he was away at the annual conference. She would just pack and go. She would find the strength because if not now then never, and her life would be over. All that would remain would be a grey future of depression and failure and fear; always the fear chewing away at her insides…

The metal gates clanged and she turned her face to the hills. How poetic that sounded, but it was necessity, not glamour, taking her left instead of right. The road to the village wound down past Mavis and Simon's house and on a bright summer day Mavis would be gardening and would want to chat. There was no time now for chat, no time for any delay.

The road to the left climbed to open moor, rounded a bend and then snaked out of sight. There was one farm with a barking dog and some cows who would no doubt glance at her with beautiful, vacant eyes. After that, nothing until the crossroads and the pub where she would wait at the bus stop.

Pauline took a deep. cleansing breath, her shoulders twitched settling the bag more comfortably and she strode on, lithe and supple. Her muscles were strong from miles and miles of hiking and from the decorating and gardening she did. Time filling; busy work that numbed her mind and squeezed out the disappointment and the sadness and the nagging, ever-present dread.

But now finally it was over. She was free. George would be away until Sunday and it was only Wednesday. Reflecting, she pushed the worry about the phone call away. It would have been sales, as usual. She mustn't panic. He wouldn't bother to ring her for a chat, they didn't have that sort of relationship; hadn't for years. What he would expect would be a clean home to come back to, a hot meal ready and her obedience in every way, even though she would detect on him the smell of his current mistress; the reek of betrayal.

The smile broadened. After all this time, she had been brave enough to get up and take back her life.

Thank heavens for Granddad. It had felt like a disappointment when her inheritance had been tied up until she was forty. George had bullied and nagged but in the end they had been unable to have the will overturned. "It will come in handy when we get it. We don't need it now and it's in a good investment plan. I'm sure Gramps meant well." The solicitor was adamant, so she had won that little battle by default. George hadn't been happy about it but there was nothing he could do except to vent his anger on her in his own inimitable, brutal way.

She raised her eyes and muttered into the warm, summer air. "Thank you, Gramps. You saved me. I don't know why you did it this way but I'm so glad you did."

The trust had matured when she turned forty. She told George it was in hand and convinced him it would be in their joint account by the end of the month. She had crossed her fingers and wagged papers at him praying that he wouldn't insist on examining them closely. He hadn't; he was wrapped up in his newest affair and spent so many nights 'working late' that he let his guard slip, convinced he had it all under control. It had been scary – so much depended on fooling him – but it was over…

But now she had won.

She gave a little skip. He wouldn't find her. By the time he came back from Edinburgh she would be long gone. In spite of herself she glanced behind her, down the road that would bring him home. What if the conference finished early? What if he was unwell and came back? Everything – the whole thing – depended on his being away until the weekend. Her stomach clenched, the urge to run now was overwhelming.

It was fine. It was all fine. He wasn't coming, she had judged it right.

The cottage on the coast was booked and there was no reason for him to ever think of the little out-of-the-way place she had chosen in Cornwall. After that it was France and the lovely place in the countryside, already hers, bought online. It had been a massive risk but desperation made her brave at last. The rest of the money would keep things ticking over a good while and by the time she needed to earn some more, then the holiday flats would be set up. Thank God for school French and for Google information and hours and hours alone in the house. It was thrilling and scary and wonderful.

She glanced at her watch. Three hours until the bus was due at the country stop. A car sped past, heading towards the village. She turned her face away, just in case. She hadn't recognised the vehicle. It was going far too fast for the narrow road, probably an outsider.

As she breasted the brow of the hill a frown wrinkled her forehead. "Oh no!" A motor bike was slewed across the road. Deep gouges scarred the black surface and the body of a sheep lying in a thickening pool of blood painted a picture that was all too clear.

Where the hell was the rider?

He must be in the ditch. She leapt forward. The sheep was quite dead, thank heavens. It was one less thing to cope with but where the hell was the rider? She ran along the side of the road peering down into the water weed and grass. He must be here somewhere! Unless he had come off and been lucky enough to walk away? No, if that was the case then he would surely have moved the bike. The sheep carcass might be beyond many people but the bike was lying across the highway, leaking petrol and oil.

She darted back and forth across the narrow road. There! She spotted him dumped in the ditch like a broken doll. Tripping and sliding she scrambled down the embankment into the cold trickle of water at the bottom. Her hiking boots would keep the water out but she had to kneel to reach the motionless body. Cold seeped through the knees of her blue, linen trousers. She reached a hand towards him. *Oh shit don't let him be dead.* "Hello, hello, can you hear me?"

Chapter 2

He was cold. The ditch water was chilly despite the heat of the day. The rider had landed with his legs in the muddy mess and his torso and head against the bank. She knew she mustn't move him and mustn't take off the safety helmet. The leather of his jacket was stiff as she pushed back the sleeve. She knew where to look for a pulse and as she felt the faint but regular beat Pauline weakened with relief.

She slipped a hand into her trouser pocket. "Shit." The phone was sitting on the table in the hall.

The man shivered and groaned. On the one hand this was a huge relief but out here in the middle of nowhere she needed medical aid quickly. His mobile was the only option. He must have one, everyone had one. "Sorry, I'm sorry." Although she didn't think he could hear her, an apology came automatically to her lips as she reached for the pockets in his jeans. They were torn, how odd that the stress of the accident had done that – the white lining was flapping out at one side. She felt in the cold water, perhaps his phone had flown out. Would it be ruined by the fall, the water? It wasn't there anyway so she must think again. Tears fell across her cheeks, tears of fear and shock and frustration but she had to ignore them. Tears wouldn't help him.

She pushed back and lifted her head to peer over the top of the ditch. Her glance skittered across the grassy bank and the roadway. He had been thrown a long way. One of his gloves was lying between them and the bike but no phone.

Panic threatened. She beat it back.

She leaned to him patting and rooting, he must have a phone. A tiny cable snaked from the side of his helmet and down into a slim pocket at the top of his jacket. "Yes." She dragged out the Nokia and unplugged the helmet device.

She was still in familiar territory and gave clear directions to the ambulance service. The dispatcher asked the obvious questions. Was he breathing? – Yes. Was his airway clear? – Yes. Was he conscious? – No. Was he bleeding? – Not as far as she could see but he was shivering now and groaning. They told her to keep him warm.

She scrambled up to the road and dragged out her jacket. Back in the ditch she tucked it round him, careful to keep it out of the water. It wouldn't be warming if it was damp. She thought he tried to open his eyes. "Hello. Can you hear me?" No response. "I'm Pauline, you're okay. The ambulance is coming." She didn't know whether he could hear but it helped to talk to him and draw some strength from the sound of her own voice.

The birds had been quiet when she first came across the scene but now they had begun to call and sing. It was surreal to sit in a wet ditch holding the hand of a stranger and sending out fearful wishes for him not to die. Waiting and praying for the ambulance to be quick and the whole horrible episode to be over while above her the birds sang into the great basin of blue sky and bees buzzed in the blossom lining the roadside.

"My name's Pauline. I have just come down the road. I think you might be hurt so you need to keep still." There was still no response but she kept going. Maybe he could hear her. Maybe it would help him to know that he wasn't alone. "I don't normally come down here in the middle of the day. It gets too hot. Not enough shade on the roadside. Mind you, perhaps that's a good thing. It would have been awful if you'd hit a tree.

"The sheep is dead. Don't feel bad, they wander all over the road, there are some killed every year. I expect the farmer will claim on his insurance.

"The ambulance shouldn't be long. I think it's about twenty minutes from town. I've asked them to hurry. The lady at the other end told me to keep talking to her but your phone battery is flat now.

"I was leaving. I was leaving my husband. That's how come I was here today. I'm starting a whole new life.

"I wish I knew your name."

He groaned again and she believed that he squeezed her fingers. Was he coming round? She was shocked then to find that she didn't want him to. She wanted someone else here, someone to tell him what to do and to take the responsibility.

She squeezed back.

"Lie still; don't try to move. I don't know how badly you're hurt. Just keep still. I won't leave you. I'll stay here. Try to relax."

Finally, with blessed relief she heard the siren in the distance. "Oh, they're coming. They're here. You'll be okay now."

In a flurry of movement and noise the road was filled. The ambulance and a police car screamed to a halt. Men and women in uniform placed cones and lights on the road, radios crackled. The EMT technicians clambered down the grassy bank.

"Hello, love. Are you okay? I'm Dave. We'll look after him now. Do you know him? Hey steady, steady. Chris, help this lady, will you?"

The relief and withdrawal of adrenalin swept her from her feet and as the world spun, darkness crawled in from the edges to take her away...

"Put your head down, love, just put your head down." She was sitting at the roadside, her head lowered between her knees, a strong arm around her shoulders and calm words whispering into her ears. The buzzing and blackness receded and her stomach heaved. "It's alright love, take some deep breaths. Everything is going to be okay now."

Slowly she lifted her head. The ambulance man was crouched beside her smiling. "You've done a great job. What's your name, love?"

"Pauline, I'm Pauline. Is he alright? He was wet... his legs. I didn't know what to do. I didn't move him but his legs were wet."

"Well, Pauline, you've done a good thing here today. Better wet legs than useless legs eh? You did just the right thing. Well done." He wrapped a silver blanket around her tucking it tightly under her arms. "You've had a bit of a shock but you'll be right as rain in a minute or two. We are sending for the air ambulance for our friend in the ditch, just in case he has back injuries. We'll look after him, don't you worry. When you've had a minute to pull yourself together we'll get one of the bobbies to take you home, change out of that wet blouse, eh. Back home and a nice cup of tea. Bet you'd like that, eh Pauline?"

Chapter 3

As the shivering stopped and her stomach settled Pauline shrugged off the survival blanket. All around there was activity. The crackle of radios and the calm but hurried movement of the uniforms created an urgent but controlled atmosphere on the quiet road. She watched them unload equipment from the ambulance and listened to a hum of voices behind her in the ditch.

Tiny white fluffballs sailed across the sky and she flapped away flying insects that buzzed her face. The day moved on with its business. The flurry of activity and drama just a few feet away from where she sat made barely a ripple in the greater pool of life.

"Are you okay now, Pauline?" A policewoman stood in front of her. Pauline raised her eyes and squinted in the brightness.

"Yes, I'm okay, I think. How is he?" She swept her hand in the direction of the ditch.

"He's still unconscious. They are putting him on a board to make sure they don't hurt his back and the air ambulance is on its way. They're giving him oxygen and fluids. They're just doing their thing you know."

Pauline nodded.

"About you though. First of all, thanks for everything you did; you may well have saved his life. Not many people come this way during the week and he could have laid there for hours. That wouldn't have done him any good at all."

"Oh, I only did what anyone else would do and I don't know that I helped that much. I'm not good with drama."

"Well you were pretty good with this one so, as I say, thanks. Now, as soon as you're ready we can take you home. You'll want to get out of those wet trousers I bet and then once you're feeling up to it we can take a statement."

"A statement? Oh… I don't think I… erm… I mean, why do you need that?"

"It's just procedure, just so what has happened is all on record. Nothing to worry about and as I say, we can do it at home when you're more relaxed. I can take you in my car. I assume you live local; you weren't driving just now?"

"No… yes, I'm local, I… I was going to town. On the bus; that's why I was walking. Normally I'd go in the car but," she sighed, "I was walking."

"Yes, but don't you want to go home and change; maybe have a cup of tea? Perhaps you should take it easy for a while, eh?"

The woman knelt before her and took hold of Pauline's hand. She peered into her hazel eyes. "Are you sure you're feeling okay? If you like we could take you down to the hospital, let the doctor have a look at you. You've had a nasty shock. Should I give your husband a call?"

"No, I don't want that. I'm not married. It's just that… I have a train to catch, in town. I was going to the bus stop and then on the train. I'm going away. It's all booked and everything."

"Oh, I see. You're wearing rings so I assumed… well, you know?"

"No, they were my mum's. It's easier sometimes if people think you're married." Pauline twisted at the bands of gold and diamonds. It had never occurred to her to remove them. They were so much a part of her that she barely noticed them.

"Well, is there anyone we can call for you? Maybe someone to give you a lift? Someone to come to your house and help you to sort things out?"

"No, I'm not going back. I don't want to go home. I…" She knew she was beginning to gabble, felt the panic rise – making her heart pump. She took a deep breath and gulped audibly.

"Hey, hey take it easy now, Pauline. Don't get upset. Look if you really feel that you're well enough to carry on I can take you to the station. How about that?"

"Oh, would you? Yes, please yes. The train goes at half past five and I think that I still have time, don't I?"

"Well, it's only just after three now so I don't see why not. Have you got some dry clothes in your bag? Mind you I have to say that I still think you might really be better going home. Could you not re-schedule and leave tomorrow?"

"No. I really don't want to go home. I have a superstition about it. It's silly I know but I think that once you've left you know, you shouldn't go back – it's from miners in the old days. My mum's to blame." She managed a small laugh as she dragged the old wife's tale from the back of her memory. "Really I would so much rather keep on and go to the station."

The whap whap of the helicopter sounded overhead and all heads turned to the west where they could see the dragonfly shape skimming the tree tops.

"Come on, Pauline, grab your bag and climb in the back of my car. I'll stand guard and make sure nobody comes too near. You change into some dry clothes and then I'll take you to the station. We can get a cup of tea and you can give me your statement then. How would that be?"

"Brilliant. Let's do that." She reached for the outstretched hand and allowed the young woman to pull her up from the roadside.

Her mouth had dried and her hands shook and she knew it was nothing to do with the accident. She would need to be careful now, very careful indeed. They were going to ask questions and she must have her wits about her. How had the bright hope come to this – already she had lied and she never lied. Not until now.

The helicopter landed in the field behind her. She grabbed her bag and clambered into the back of the police car, ducking her head to hide the tears of panic.

Chapter 4

Pauline let her head fall back against the hard cushion. As the train slid forward and picked up speed she struggled not to cry; tried to bite back the sadness. For countless months, years now, when in deep despair, when she had felt so alone and afraid, it had been just like this. For all the weeks since her resolve had stiffened and she had found hope. All the nights when hope seemed lost and she believed her present would be her future and there was no way to go on, it had been this. Through all of it she had fantasised about, dreamed of this journey, or at least a version of it. She had held it close to her heart and it sustained her and yet now, now that it had come to be, it was a sharp and bitter disappointment.

When she had left the house just a few hours ago, the joy, the sense of freedom and achievement, had bubbled inside her. Now the overwhelming emotions were worry and shame. She had lied, over and over while they told her what a good Samaritan she was – a responsible citizen and a caring person. She had fed them untruths and subterfuge and scrambled facts.

She replayed the conversation in her mind as the scene swam across the inside of her eyelids. A steaming cup of coffee on the Formica table in the police station. The police woman sitting opposite with a glass of coke, "Are you sure you don't want something to eat Pauline?" "No, this is great." She had sipped at the hot drink and felt her physical self strengthen and then, as her nerves settled, she had begun to lie.

The surname of a friend from school, the phone number with three of the digits transposed. The address which was her mother and father's old one, though the house had been demolished and a pair of semis stood on the plot. The story that hackers had made it necessary to close all her internet accounts so no, she was sorry but she didn't have an email address. So it went, on and on.

"You probably won't hear from us again. The farmer will very likely have insurance for his sheep and the biker will claim on his. The insurance companies may get in touch though it's not certain and that would be by post. If the unthinkable happens and he doesn't pull through then it may be necessary for you to attend an inquest, but let's hope for the best, eh? Let's hope that won't happen."

She had nodded and smiled and then felt her spirit shrivel.

The police woman took her to the station and offered to help her find the platform, help her to find a seat. "No, it's fine. You've been so kind already." She couldn't let them know her destination. They shook hands and parted, and she felt traitorous and dishonest.

Now, hurtling through the pretty countryside in her comfortable seat on the train, she fought to recapture some of her earlier calm and happiness. Without doubt she had done the right thing, for there had been no other option. The man needed her help and she had given it. The rest of it; the contact with the police and the possibility of further involvement was a worry. Potentially it threatened everything. On the other hand, maybe she was simply being hysterical and paranoid. Perhaps the police were no threat at all, and didn't that make it all so much worse, for she had lied unnecessarily. What a mess.

She had planned so carefully. This was but a small part of the whole plan; a break in the UK, in a part of the country they had never visited as a couple and would not immediately suggest itself as a place to search for her.

Once he realised she had left him then George would no doubt look for her passport. When it wasn't there he would guess she had travelled abroad. If he involved the police and they feared for her safety then they would check channel crossings and airports, wouldn't they? So, she would wait, give it time before she left the country. She had been seen in the village on Monday and Tuesday so the search would be timed from after that. She had never been afraid of the police; she'd had no reason to be, not until today, until the lying. Her fear had always been simply of her husband: the idea that he might come looking for her. George would be angry and peevish so she must cover her tracks.

The house in France wouldn't be hers for a few weeks yet so there was no rush to be there. Although the sale had included some basic furniture, a lot more would be needed. Until she owned property it wasn't possible to buy a car, so one would have to be hired. She would need to find where to buy essentials for her new home. Though the prospect was thrilling it was also challenging. She would have to manage things she had never done before on her own and she had thought it might be overwhelming right on top of her escape. So, a break in Cornwall, an out-of-the-way village and a chance to stop and take stock and breathe had seemed a gentle way to start and it was a gift to herself, a reward for her bravery. A hidey hole and a refuge.

As the train rushed through the sunlit fields and sleepy villages she tried to regain control. Though things had gone awry in a totally unlooked-for way she must get back on track. It just was not possible for everything to fail so quickly so she took a deep breath. She straightened her shoulders and, from somewhere deep inside, dragged back her strength and resolve.

She would make it work and make it right. She turned to the window and watched the green fields fly past, a glimpse of a fox, the still life image of a herd of deer, and the constant flash of cars on the roads running alongside the railway. She dredged up a watery smile. It was okay. Lying was wrong, but at the end of the day the good that she had done surely outweighed the subterfuge and dishonesty.

No matter, it was all too late now and it was over. They couldn't find her, not even if they needed to, so she would put it behind her and move along. There was no other option.

Chapter 5

The smell of fish and chips; petrol fumes. Rush and dash and noise. This wasn't it; the place that she was looking for should be sea air and tar, and landed fish and the cry of gulls. Pauline shook her head. She wasn't a fool and had expected it to be a little this way but it was a disappointment nonetheless. What she wanted was the feel of new summer sandals, cotton shorts and a soft blouse. She wanted to clasp Granddad's hardened, gardener's hands as he shepherded her across the road and lifted her to the sea wall so she could walk high above the damp sand and the deck chairs and other golden children. She wanted Nana's gentle smile and her wad of tissues from her shopping bag to wipe away the sticky drool of ice cream. She was craving the safety and sureness and the feeling of being special, of being beloved.

Throughout her childhood Mum and Dad suffered guilt because they couldn't leave their business in the summer but Pauline had never minded. She was the special one, the reason for the holiday and the light in the life of her grandparents. They spoiled her and filled her days with laughter and the beach and boat rides and coach trips and made such memories that now, in this scary time she had come to find it again. It wasn't here today but it was enough that it had been once so she hefted her bag and made her way to the taxi rank.

"Porthelland please, Gull's Rest… do you know it?"

"Aye – I do. Nice day again."

"Hmm, lovely."

"Having a break are ya? Before the hordes arrive."

"The hordes?"

"Oh aye, another month you won't be able to move for tourists. Nothing wrong with it of course; my best season. But it's nice now, just before it all goes ballistic."

"Ah I see… yes it's lovely now, but busier than I remember. How far is it to Gull's Rest?"

"Oh, it's about half an hour, you sit back and enjoy the ride my dear. It'll be twenty five pounds, is that okay?"

"Oh yes, that's fine. I knew it was a little way out of town."

"Aye, it is that, but beautiful if you want some peace."

The taxi pulled out of the rank and joined the melee. Now and then a tantalising glimpse of sun on water twinkled between the buildings and there was the cry of gulls and the feeling of holiday so it wasn't all lost to burgers and booze. Pauline settled back and tried to relax…

"Here we are lovey. Gull's Rest. You've been fast asleep. You must have had a long day. It's tiring, is travellin'; one of the reasons I stays at home."

"Oh, sorry."

"No need, lovey, no need. You're on your holidays after all. Now is Jim meeting you here or is it to be Dolly?"

"I'm not sure, but I think someone is. Thanks so much."

"Oh well, best hope for Dolly!" With a little chuckle the driver helped her out and passed Pauline her bag. "Do you want to book for the return?"

"Oh, I hadn't thought about that."

"Here you go, here's my card. You just give me a ring and it'll be cheaper if you pre-book." With a wink and a little smile the taxi driver turned his face away and rumbled out of the small cobbled yard.

Pauline took a deep breath. Yes, there it was now; what she had come here for. The salt tang and the smell of warm dust and new cut grass and behind that the farm smells… and at last she felt a knot inside begin to unwind.

The sky was losing brightness and colouring down through a fading blue to the magic shades of a sun kissed evening. Swifts and swallows looped and bent above her and she could hear the buzz of a motor boat out on the water. This was close to heaven, surely.

The old door on the little cottage swung open and a round man of indeterminate age stepped across the narrow patch of grass. Pauline smiled at him and held out her hand.

"Oh so, you're here at last. I don't normally 'spect to be this late. Past dinner and me still waiting here. Could you not get an earlier train?"

"Oh, erm… sorry. I didn't think there was a schedule."

"No, no, probl'y not. Nobody thinks I might have something else to do. Holiday for one bain't be holiday for all. I have cows to see to and me sittin' waiting. Well, you're here now. Come in if you're comin'."

It was pretty funny; she bit back the urge to chuckle. The booking online had given the impression that this was a sleek modern organisation, and yet here was this curmudgeonly farmer stomping back towards the beautiful little house and ducking under the low lintel. *Oh well, onward and upward, Pauline.*

"Right. Here be the livin' room. Upstairs, beds. Kitchen through here."

She dropped her bag in the small, dim hallway and hurried through to the bright little kitchen. It was spotless. The worktops were white tile and the wooden cupboard units and Belfast sink obviously part of a new refurbishment that had been done with care and love. Yellow curtains shifted in the evening air and beyond the small back garden and stone wall there was a rough meadow and then there was the sea. Diamantes danced and twinkled as the great body of water heaved and shifted under the orange ball of the sun sliding towards the horizon. It literally took her breath away.

"You've plenty time to stare at water. I need to get on."

She turned and Jim was stood behind her holding a sheaf of papers. "Here be instructions. Washer, dish machine, cooker. Try not to break 'em. Should be no problem with drains and stuff: all redone last winter. Sick to death of dashin' up here all hours for blockages. The stuff people think they can flush away! Makes my blood boil.

"You've ordered a welcome pack."

She felt the laughter welling again at the word from this dour old farmer's lips but she held her peace and painted a smile on her face. "There's bacon 'n eggs, there's bread 'n butter and a bit o' cheese. There's tea and suchlike. I 'spect you'll want wine. Every bugger wants wine. Well there bain't be wine but there's a bottle o' beer and a pub down the road. They'll sell you bottles of wine if you've money to burn on such stuff.

"Now then. Do you want cleanin'?"

"Sorry?"

"Cleanin'. Do ya want cleanin'? Every other mornin' Dolly can come in."

"Oh, yes please. That would be lovely."

"Aye, well, maybe. You're booked for a week so this time next Wednesday you need to be gone."

"Is it booked up after that?"

"What?"

"The cottage… is it booked for the week after? If I wanted to stay longer would it be possible?"

21

"Aye, I daresay. I'll send Dolly in the mornin'. Cows be waitin'. Here be keys."

And that was it. He pulled the door closed behind him and she could hear him calling as he stomped off down the road. "Here Barney, get here ya bugger." She could only assume Barney was a dog that she hadn't seen.

It started deep inside. Some of it was relief and a hint of hysteria but a great part was simply confounded amusement at the strange welcome. Each time she ran through the greetings the giggle caused her to catch her breath until in the end she was chuckling loudly. In the fading light of the Cornish evening she recaptured the pleasure of the morning when she had slammed the door on her past. It had been a long and difficult day but see now: she had coped and she was here and yes, she felt happier than she had for a long, long time. She didn't need wine because the joy in her heart was now so intoxicating.

Chapter 6

Whether it was the long sleep in the taxi, residual tension, or the unfamiliar surroundings, Pauline didn't float into the dreamless sleep that she had hoped for.

After a supper of omelette, fresh bread and a glass of beer, she felt nicely drowsy. With the windows and doors of the little cottage closed, the lullaby of the ocean was a gentle whisper. The house was comfortably warm and as she slipped between fresh smelling sheets in the double bedroom she felt relaxed and ready for bed.

There were no bumps or lumps in the mattress and the pillows were soft. Moonlight slid through a tiny gap in the curtain and drew a line across the bed and up the wall. The tiny spear of silver was a comfort in the otherwise total darkness. She stretched her legs full length. She curled into a ball on her side. She lay on her back, then turned onto her stomach yet still the sleep she so wanted refused to come. After almost an hour the sheets were wrinkled and creased and the nerves in her legs were jumping and twitching.

The house creaked and popped as old wood and warm stone cooled but she wasn't afraid, not at all. She was simply sleepless. Out on the tiny landing there was a night light plugged into a wall socket, it was enough to find her way downstairs without the need for the overhead lamp. Although she would rather have been asleep the realisation had come that in fact it didn't matter. She had no-one to answer to and no responsibilities the next day. For the first time in many years her life was her own to do with as she pleased.

She could spend the whole night gazing from the window across the dark meadow to the ocean where breaking waves shone in the moonlight. If she chose to curl up in the window seat sipping tea and listening to the owl and nightjar and cows, which would low occasionally from nearby, it didn't matter to anyone but her. For at long last she was free. After sitting in the living room for a while eating chocolate biscuits and drinking tea and relishing the feeling of guilty pleasure she made her way into the kitchen to rinse her cup. The garden was now all dappled grey shapes with just one blaze of white where a rose climbed on a trellis beside the wall.

Of course she would go to the beach tomorrow if the weather was fine. Through the tiny gate in the old stone wall and down to the warm sand and the glittering water. Now, in the night standing by the kitchen window she wondered what it would be like to go immediately. To make her way through the dark rustle of the meadow, to follow the sandy path and then walk in bare feet along the wet sand with the cold water lapping at her ankles. She didn't know the way yet, hadn't had a chance to explore but she promised herself that before she left there would be a walk down in the darkness and a walk along the moon-washed shore.

* * *

She didn't realise that she had slept until she woke to the chaotic cheep and chatter of birds. There was an occasional whoosh of car tyres on the road outside and knocking on the front door. She slid from the bed and leaned to open the leaded window. "Hello. I'm up here."

"Oh, sorry my dear. I thought you might be out. I'm Dolly. I brought milk." The slim woman dressed in light trousers and a bright flower-patterned blouse lifted a bottle as evidence.

"I didn't mean to disturb you, dear. Shall I just leave it here?"

"No, no it's fine. I think I've overslept. Hang on I'll come down."

She glanced down at her wrinkled pyjamas and shrugged. The woman knew she had been in bed, but what did it matter? She ran down the stairs and dragged open the front door.

"Come in please. What time is it? I didn't get off to sleep until late."

"It's only eight my dear. Was there something wrong with the bed?"

"No, nothing like that. I think I was just overtired. I'm Pauline." She held out a hand but the woman mistook the gesture and plonked the milk bottle in her curled fingers.

"Oh, right. Thanks."

"So, I'm Dolly and Jim said you might want cleaning and maybe to stay a bit longer than you've booked for?"

"Yes, well yes to the cleaning and to be honest I think I would like to stay. My plans right now are flexible and it's so lovely here. I haven't been since I was little and I'd forgotten how peaceful it is."

"Well, I can come in every other day. I'll bring you milk and if you let me know whether you want bread or anything, I can order it for you. There is a shop in the village. That's about twenty five minutes' walk and they have most of the essentials, though we do sell vegetables here. We have a butcher who comes twice a week and the pub down the road does meals."

"Have you got time for a cup of tea, coffee?"

"That would be nice. I can't stay long but a cup of coffee would be really nice, thank you. I hope Jim wasn't too grumpy with you. I don't like asking him to do the opening up but my friend's daughter has just had a baby and I was up there all day helping her."

Pauline looked at the woman, she was late middle aged, with well-cut brown hair flecked a little grey around the temples. She was dressed casually but neatly and seemed to be wearing just a little understated make up. This person was totally unlike the Dolly she would have imagined as partner to the cranky Jim of the previous night.

"Well, he was… erm… a little disturbed, I think because I was later than he expected."

"Oh dear, I'm sorry. He's my brother and we run the place together. My hubby died a while ago and I moved back here. The farm was my dad's and it's Jim's really now and I just run the guest side of things and the vegetable shop."

"Oh, it's okay, it had been a funny day anyway and he wasn't rude." With her tongue firmly in her cheek Pauline had decided she liked this woman and didn't want to embarrass her. After all, the strange welcome had in the end lifted her mood.

"Well, if you need anything just let me know and if you do speak to Jim just take him as you find him. He's as good as gold really."

"You don't have as strong an accent as your brother."

"No, I lived near London while I was married. I taught up there, it's nice to be back though."

Pauline clattered round the kitchen filling the kettle and searching for cups and coffee. When the drink was made Dolly opened the back door.

"It's a lovely morning, do you mind if we sit out here. There's a little table and we can watch the water. I did miss it when I was away and I can sit and watch it for hours."

"Oh, yes that would be lovely. Can I book for an extra time, maybe another ten days on top of the week I already paid for?"

"Yes, I should think that's fine. I'll check the book and if there's a problem I'll let you know. Have you got your mobile number?"

"Oh, crikey. Yes, that was one of the things that happened yesterday you see. I lost my phone." Another lie joined the tangle and already this new relationship was tinged with small guilt. "I'll have to order one, the booking form said you have wi-fi... is that right?"

"Yes, you should be able to get a signal in any room and even out here if you're in luck. I can pop back if there's a problem; otherwise I'll make the booking. Anyway, I'll leave you to get on. I hope you have a nice stay and anything you need just let us know. Are you a writer or a painter or..."

"No, no. Why do you ask?"

"Oh, it's just that usually people who come on their own, they're arty types wanting peace to work. It's none of my business of course but I just wondered you know."

"Oh, I see. No, I've been through a bit of a stressful time and I just thought a break would do me good; you know, a change of scene. I'm used to being on my own." As she said it Pauline didn't feel the little tug of guilt; this at least wasn't entirely a lie as she felt that she had in an emotional sense been on her own for years. She had always hidden the problems of her marriage, even from her friends. She had felt so lonely for so long, even when George was in the room with her, because there was such a chasm of dislike and distrust between them that was impossible to bridge.

Dolly, perhaps noticing that Pauline was rather distracted by her thoughts, quietly took her cup back into the kitchen. "You sit there and enjoy the sun, my dear, I'll let myself out." And with a flap of her hand to wave goodbye she was gone. Pauline leaned back against the wooden bench and watched the gulls follow a fishing boat, diving into the white wake and screaming with excitement in the clear morning.

Chapter 7

First things first. Pauline logged on with her MacBook and ordered a new phone. Then she picked out some clothes. What she had managed to bring with her would do for a few days but now she had achieved the first part of the journey, she would be able to handle more luggage. Her wardrobes had been full but she wanted none of the wrappings of that downtrodden and lonely woman. She felt no regret for leaving behind her the soft armour of gowns worn to events she had never enjoyed. Nor for the sweaters and skirts with invisible stains of violence and hurt which were gone from the fabric but still vivid in her mind.

After toast and more coffee while she surfed and shopped she left the cottage and headed down the narrow road towards the village. The embankments were high and overgrown with tall grasses and wildflowers. The dopey murmur of bees and the zip of smaller insects filled her ears and the frantic scuttering as smaller creatures fled punctuated the regular slap, slap of her shoes on the hot tarmac. Once or twice she had to make sure she walked very close to the bank to avoid oncoming traffic and she found herself wondering how the injured rider was doing back in the hospital.

She bought some bits and pieces at the little supermarket and with a quiet chuckle picked up a couple of bottles of wine from their small selection, after all *every bugger wants wine,* don't they?

As is the way of these things the walk back seemed shorter and in little more than an hour she was back in the garden drinking cold orange juice and clicking through the online editions of the papers. At first she found nothing and assumed that no news was good news. Surely if the man were dead it would be mentioned somewhere and then she spotted a tiny article. It reported simply that 'yet another' sheep related accident had put a motorbike rider in hospital and posed the question, 'When was something going to be done about the animals wandering loose along the roadsides?' The rider wasn't identified and when the article was published he was simply in hospital in a serious condition. So, not dead then. Well, not at eight thirty that morning, but it still didn't sound good. No matter; even if the police did try to find her again she was sure that the obfuscation had been enough to cover her tracks.

The endless blue of sky and sea curved in a great arc before her. Warm sun stroked her shoulders, easing the tension and smoothing away the worry. The drama of yesterday was a world and a lifetime since and she would let it go…

The narrow road beyond the farm was dusty with a messy mixture of earth and sharp sand. Pauline followed in the footsteps of the small caravan of holiday makers who trod this way most of the morning. The dunes seemed higher now she was amongst them. The long grass whispered and sang and called her on towards the louder melody of the ocean and then there it was. Dancing white waves and heaving billows of deep blue and sapphire and violet. She paused and gloried in the vision. Wind whipped and pulled at her hair. Sounds of children and gulls were whisked past her ears and on and away into the ether. She filled her lungs and eyes with it and let her mind whirl into the past, when the beach meant nothing but pleasure; sun tightened skin and the cold shock of a run through breaking surf.

Slipping and slithering she came through the dunes and onto the light sand and then the line of pebbles at the tide line. She slipped off her sandals and felt the squidge of sandy mud between her toes and she grinned. This was truly wonderful. George had never liked the beach and after several tries early in their marriage she had given up the fight and now realised just how much she had missed this wild, warm, wonderful world.

A tiny recess in the rocks offered shelter and she leaned against the warm hardness and shuffled her bottom into a comfortable place. She heaved a great sigh. The distant sounds of pleasure tickled at the edges of hearing and the soughing of the vegetation in the dunes was mesmerising. She laid her head back against the stone and closed her eyes.

Drifting and drowsing she started visibly when a quiet voice invaded her peace. "Penny for your thoughts? They must be nice if the expression on your face is anything to go by!"

"Oh, Dolly! Hello!"

"Sorry if I disturbed you."

"No, it's fine. I was almost asleep and that wouldn't be a good idea really. I haven't put on any sunscreen yet. I hate the stickiness."

"Yes, me too, but they tell us we have to do it, don't they? I saw you there and thought I'd just pop up and let you know I booked you in for the extra time and I'll be in tomorrow morning to tidy for you."

"Lovely, thanks. Can I order some milk and a loaf? I'll pop in later and buy some salad."

"Great. And we have some really lovely strawberries just arrived; do you want me to put some aside for you?"

"Oh yes please."

"Well, I'll leave you in peace. I'll be in the vegetable shop until about six tonight. I'll see you later on then."

As the other woman trudged away through the soft sand Pauline was suddenly swept up by a feeling of loneliness. She had said she was used to being alone and this was true, but that didn't mean that she was always happy about it. However, it was easier than pretending all was well when it was far from being so. It was easier than making up stories about falls that hadn't happened and cupboard doors that were in fact innocent of causing anyone any harm. To have someone though, who you could trust to chat with, was such an innocent thing and she wondered how she had allowed herself to become so very cut off from all her old friends. A bubble of panic roiled in her stomach. She was going away to a country where she knew no-one and where, though she felt confident in her language skills, she would be unfamiliar with the customs of daily life. Had she made a stupid mistake? Had the desperate need to escape led her to flee too far and too fast?

Chapter 8

"Hello, Pauline. I've finished now. You didn't really need me to come in did you? There was nothing out of place. Three days already and the place is as tidy as it was when you arrived. I'm not going to charge you for today."

"Oh no, that's not right! I asked you to come. To be honest I didn't realize how much I'd be out. I've been at the beach so much and I've had lovely long walks that I haven't been around enough to trash the place." Pauline smiled at Dolly across the room. "Do you want a cup of coffee? I was just going to make one. Do you have time?"

"Oh lovely, yes. I usually have one when I get home anyway so that'd be great. Look, I'll tell you what, I usually charge for an hour, so why don't I come in for half an hour on Monday and I'll lump the two together. Then we can decide what to do for the next couple of weeks. I don't want to take advantage. Usually people who come down with children have all sorts of mess to clear up, sand everywhere and toys, you know. I don't mind it at all, it's important people enjoy their stay."

"Oh Dolly, that's very kind of you. You know when I leave here I'm going to be running a holiday place myself.

More of a bed and breakfast to start with, but then I'm hoping to have a barn converted into flats."

"Oh well, the best of luck. It's hard work but it's lovely when the people are nice. Some of them are quite difficult to deal with, mind you. Is it in Cornwall, your place? Are we going to be business rivals?" Dolly winked as she pulled a chair out from under the kitchen table and snagged a biscuit from the plate.

"No, I'm buying a place in France."

"On your own?"

"Yes," Pauline grimaced as she nodded her head. "Eeek and all that!"

"Wow! Well you're very brave."

"My granddad left me some money and I thought, well, if I don't do it now I never will so there we are. I have to say I'm nervous but excited as well."

"So… when is this happening?"

"The house will be mine in about another month and I'm planning to be there for a couple of weeks before that."

"Are you selling up here then?"

Oh why had she blurted out the information? Now she was going to have to back pedal and smudge the truth again.

No, she wouldn't.

"Actually, my ex-husband has the house here. He's keeping that."

"Oh, sorry. I didn't mean to pry."

"No, it's fine." She leaned forward and touched a finger to Dolly's hand where it curled around her steaming mug. "Really, it's fine. All that is in the past and I'm moving on."

"Well good for you."

A knot of nerves fluttered deep in her belly as the words rolled from her lips. On the one hand it was all true, but in reality George didn't even know that she'd gone yet. What would his reaction be, as the days and weeks rolled on? She couldn't think that far, couldn't even guess what he would do. Maybe in the dim and distant future, when she was strong and secure, she could get a solicitor and arrange a divorce. For now it was enough to be away from him. She pushed the darkness aside and smiled at Dolly. "Anyway, that's why I'm spoiling myself a bit. I think it's the last chance I'll get for a while."

Dolly smiled gently. "So then. Are you enjoying your stay so far?"

"I am. I'm going out for another long walk later and then tonight I have a treat planned."

"Oh right, are you going into the village? To the bistro? You need to book on Saturdays you know, I can give them a ring if you like?"

"No, nothing like that. I'm going to take a bottle of wine and go down on the beach and walk in the surf in the moonlight! You'll think I'm mad but ever since I saw the silver glow on that first night I've wanted to do it."

"Down on the beach? At night on your own?"

"Yes, you like the beach, don't you? I bet you've done it loads of times!"

"Well yes, I love the beach, certainly. And I go down there every day if I can. I missed it so much when we lived up near London and now I can't get enough of it. But not at night."

"Not at night?"

"No, not me."

"It's not illegal or something is it?"

"No, no of course not. It's just that we don't. Nobody does, not at night."

"But why; it looks beautiful."

"Yes, from here, from a distance I dare say it does but… well you know Cornwall, these beaches, this coastline. It has a dark and violent history. Things have happened over time that have left a mark on the land."

A mark on the land. If it hadn't been for the serious, almost fearful expression in the other woman's eyes Pauline would have laughed, but as it was she simply tipped her head to one side and waited for more information.

"I know it sounds melodramatic and everything. It's probably just old wives' tales and stories to frighten children but… well… we just don't. Now and again people have done and then they just stopped."

"Why? Why do they stop?"

"Oh look, I'm being silly. If you want to go down on the beach then that's what you should do. Thanks so much for the coffee. Enjoy your day, my dear. Take care."

Well that was odd. Pauline had taken the landlady for a level headed, down-to-earth woman and the strange conversation left her puzzled. Her nerves were on edge anyway; tomorrow George would be home and she couldn't help thinking about what his reaction was going to be when he found her gone.

She shook her head, rinsed the mugs, and then turned to pick up her shoulder bag. She strode out of the house and off towards the cliff top walk. Maybe she would just stay in the cottage tonight and read her book. Tomorrow night she would go to the beach. Yes, she'd leave it until tomorrow.

Chapter 9

Sunday morning. Warmth oozed into the bedroom and outside the window, birdsong and distant squeals of children on their way to the beach told her it was not early. Pauline pulled the duvet over her head and squeezed her eyelids tightly together. It was Sunday. Today George was to arrive home. She played the scenes through in her mind.

He would come in through the front door and throw his case down in the hallway. There would be no greeting, no friendly call out to her for he hadn't ever expected she would leave what she was doing to greet him. He would fling his keys into the brass bowl in the hall. In the past that would have given her an idea of his mood. If they slammed against the metal causing it to ring and chime then she would take herself through to the lounge and curl into the chair in the corner, giving him space. If they jingled gently as he lowered them into the basin then she would put the kettle on for a cup of coffee and thank her lucky stars that the meetings had gone well or whichever woman he had been with had been pliant and undemanding and left him satisfied.

She acknowledged a long time ago that it was pathetic for her life to be governed by these unknown sisters but there had been no alternative.

Today though, what would he think? What would he do? What conclusion would he draw from the empty silence? Perhaps he would storm from room to room calling her name? No doubt he would go back outside and double check the car port to see if her car was still there. She imagined him slamming into the kitchen where there would be no aroma of a carefully prepared meal and no wine open to breathe on the work top.

She pushed aside the duvet and wriggled up on the pillows.

Would he worry? Phone calls to friends would embarrass him. They were all his friends anyway. She had lost touch with hers when the bruises became too regular and the explanations for them weaker, the ugly truth increasingly obvious. Neighbours, golf couples would all tell him no, Pauline wasn't with them. No, they hadn't seen her, not for a few days now that they considered it.

How long would it be before he realised that the autofeeder for the cat had been set and would, by now, be empty. For a moment her eyes filled when she thought of Samson; how she loved him. She knew that George was as sentimental as she when it came to the old tom. Whatever else he did, he would take care of the cat. Probably one of the first things that he would do would be to empty the litter tray and open a tin of tuna. By that time, surely he would know that something had happened.

Then what? Would he call hospitals, the police? Or would he make a sandwich and pour himself a drink and sit and fume and plan his revenge for when she did come home?

She slid her feet out from under the covers. Today was going to be difficult. She expected to feel on edge and nervy but… it must be lived. Lived and consigned to her history.

The cottage garden was bright and welcoming when she made her way downstairs. Trees swayed in the sea breeze and, as she drank her coffee, sparrows niggled and fought over the bread crumbs she scattered on the grass. Twinkling in the near distance the ocean called to her, tempted her, but her soul was uneasy.

Watching young couples playing in the waves and the families enjoying the weekend treat of a trip to the coast held no appeal today. Though she was proud and pleased to have made the break, her heart was still sad that her marriage had failed. All her young dreams had been crushed by cruelty and meanness. The bright young couple had become part of a sad statistic.

"Hello, are you in the garden?"

"Oh, Dolly, hello. I've just made a pot of coffee; do you want one?"

"Yes please. I'm not disturbing you, am I?"

"No, it's lovely to see you. I'm having trouble getting going today. I haven't made my mind up what I'm going to do yet."

"I'm just on my way now down to the village. It's the craft fair on the green today and I didn't know whether or not you'd seen the notices. It's a nice day out. Gates open at twelve, you can get something to eat – well if you like hog roast, hot dogs that sort of thing, and there's a beer tent and a cake and coffee corner. If you've nothing to do why don't you pop down? For once we've got a lovely day for it and there's nice bits and pieces of craft for sale and all the proceeds go into the village fund for the school and the village hall and so on. Don't feel obliged – I just thought I'd let you know."

"Oh right, well I might pop down later."

"Are you alright? You seem a bit down?"

"Oh, I guess I have a lot on my mind today and it's making me a bit unsettled. A village fete sounds just the sort of thing to take me out of myself."

"Now, it's not the fete, that's in September but it's a lovely day in any case."

"Excellent. Thanks so much, Dolly."

"Pauline…"

"Yes?"

"Did you go to the beach the other night? You know you said that you were thinking of going down in the dark, did you?"

"No, I didn't as a matter of fact."

"Ah, I just wondered if that was why you were feeling unsettled. Maybe you had gone down and perhaps – well, not enjoyed it."

"No, I will go though. Does it worry you, the idea of me down there?"

"Oh, don't take any notice of me. It's silly old stories and when you grow up with them they are just part of life I suppose."

"But, what are they, these stories?"

"Well… now I don't want to put you off doing something you want to, but… there is a story about a ghost roaming the cliffs and beaches at night. I know it's probably rubbish but some people reckon that if they've stayed until it's got dark that they've seen a figure on the headland and it's spooked them. There's nothing to it really, I'm sure… but not many people like to go down there. Do you believe in that sort of thing? Spirits, ghosts and such like?"

"I'm not sure to be honest. Anyway, I'm sure no ghost will be interested in me, will they? I'm only a visitor after all!"

"Yes, I'm sure you're right. Oh, there's the car. Jim is taking me down. I have some cakes to take with me. I'll watch out for you later. Thanks for the coffee."

"Yes, I'll see you later. Bye Dolly."

The company had cheered her and now that the day had a shape and substance to it her mood lifted. George would surely sneak into her thoughts now and again but

40

when she considered him it was with a flush of pride at her actions and not a little buzz of – well what? – yes, that was it; a feeling of revenge…

* * *

It was old fashioned and easy and charming. She roamed around the field, drank warm wine in a tent that smelled of damp canvas and remembered her distant past. She allowed her mind to bask in the remembered happiness of childhood and as the day wound down, felt grateful for whatever instinct had led her here, where childhood memories were pleasant and the joy was simple.

All would be well.

She leaned back in a plastic chair and closed her eyes. Noise buzzed and flowed around her, blending into a pleasant hum. Sun warmed her face. She relaxed.

Then suddenly from nowhere a sliver of unease trickled down her back and she shivered. She opened her eyes and rubbed at the goose bumps on her arms. A movement at the corner of the beer tent then caught her eye. A dark shape was moving quickly away. She was fully awake now. The tension of the day was getting to her and it was time to go back to the cottage. She pushed up from the chair and made away across the field, the smell of crushed grass and warm wood filled her senses as she regained her equilibrium.

The road was quiet in the gathering evening with just the distant cry of the gulls and the regular beat of her feet on the tarmac. She heard an approaching car and moved closer to the hedge. It slowed as it drew nearer. She felt the rumble as it rolled alongside and glanced back; it was close, very close. She clambered up onto the steep verge and grabbed at a branch to steady herself. The bulk of it was level with her now. The windows were tinted and all she had managed had been a glimpse of a dark shape at the wheel. Her heart thumped as the vehicle came almost to a standstill. Her stomach tightened with nerves and then, with a roar it sped away and on into the distance. She shook her head, some people were so thoughtless, and now she had prickled her hands on brambles and her trouser hems were stained from mud in the gutter. She should have taken the licence number. As the thought crossed her mind she acknowledged that it would have been meaningless. Nothing had happened, not really.

It was late afternoon and the day was almost over. She hopped back to the firmness of the road and strode on towards the cottage. A huge landmark had been reached. Now that he must know for sure that she had gone, the freedom seemed more real, more final. It was good, it felt really good.

Chapter 10

Sunday was gone, and in the event it had been easier than Pauline had anticipated. The spectre of unfinished business had nibbled at her subconscious and now she could put it behind her.

It was Monday. By now George would know for sure that something real, something final had taken place. Whether or not the police were involved didn't matter anymore. Down here beside the ocean in this quiet spot she felt sure that she was well hidden. Although the events of the week had replayed in her mind repeatedly, she could see no way that anyone could trace her.

From today the rest of life was before her. The morning felt warm and bright and the cliff walk tempted her out into the sunshine.

She was free and untrammelled and rather surprised that she simply didn't care what happened to George from here on. His brutality and selfishness had killed any affection she had for him. He could wallow now in confusion and disarray as he tried to find his way around the kitchen; the washing machine, the cooker. It was unlikely that any of his female playmates would be interested in his dirty laundry or his empty belly and perhaps he would miss her. But she didn't want to be missed because his shirts were crumpled in the bottom of the laundry hamper or because lettuce wilted and stank in the fridge. She knew he wouldn't miss her for her arms or her smile or her loving because they had been gone from his life for such a long time. He had wasted them and cast them aside so, whether he pined or forgot, she no longer wanted to know.

Long grass swayed in waves beside her, an echo of the rolling blue beyond the cliffs. Gulls screeched and dived against the brilliant sky and her spirits soared with them.

It was time to plan and organise. She gave a little skip and then, feeling foolish, glanced behind to make sure no-one had seen.

Two hours of walking left her well exercised and her limbs warmed and loose. She took a sandwich out into the garden with a glass of orange juice and set up her MacBook. She would contact the agent about the house. It was time for him to have her new email address. In preparation for her flight she had set up the new contact details and felt confident that nothing unexpected had happened. Buying a house in France did seem so much less stressful than in England with the date agreed well in advance and no chance of a last minute change of heart or nasty alteration in price.

She sent off the message and brought up the pictures of the place she was buying. It was old but had already been modernised. She knew her limitations and although gardening and decorating were well within her capabilities, building work was not. For the first few months the four extra bedrooms could be let and the agent had been very helpful with information about how to obtain all the necessary permits and so on. And then there was the barn. Excitement fluttered in her stomach and anticipation widened her grin as she looked at the images. She had already had a surveyor take a look and pronounce it sound and suitable for conversion. It would make four holiday flats. There was already a pool and a big garden with mature trees and she had plans to make a tiny but beautiful holiday location. It would take time but she had it, didn't she? Thanks to Granddad she had the money and she had her freedom. She wrapped her arms around her waist and rocked slightly, holding herself in a hug. She felt so very blessed right then, so very lucky.

Her eyes swept the gorgeous vista in front of her. She would miss England of course but it wasn't that far away. She could fly in a little over an hour from several different airports so if she ever felt the need to come back, it was simple. For now, though, she would enjoy the next couple of weeks, treat herself to some real relaxation and then be more than ready for the challenges – she would welcome them.

Tomorrow she would go back into Newquay, have a lavish lunch and a walk around the shops but today she would spend in the garden with her book and then tonight, maybe tonight she would go down to the beach in the moonlight.

Chapter 11

The weather turned wet and stormy so Pauline's adventure in the darkness didn't happen. She filled her time with walks and reading and chats with Dolly who now came most mornings for a cup of coffee either in the garden or the bright little kitchen. Although she was frustrated, she put the beach walk on hold until conditions were perfect.

Thursday was bright and warm. As the sun dipped in a blaze of crimson against a turquoise sky she left the house to make her way down to the deserted beach. She took off her sandals and her feet sank into the warm powder below the dunes. Slipping and slithering between the hillocks and then down across the flatness she reached where the wet sand gleamed in the darkness. Her toes wiggled in the rolling wavelets. The sensation of cold wetness underfoot and warm swirling water tickling her ankles felt odd and she savoured the strangeness.

She spun to face the way that she had come. The lights in the cottage shone in the darkness and beyond that the farm was lit by the lamp at the entrance and the muted glow from rooms behind closed curtains.

Pauline threw back her head. The moon was a little more than a thumbnail and the dark velvet of the night sky was scattered with countless silver pinpricks. It was mystical and she felt small and insignificant but at the same time so much a part of the universe that it brought tears to her eyes and a warmth deep in her heart.

Out on the dark water the lights of trawlers bobbed and danced in the swell and the sound of an engine throbbed at the very edge of her hearing. It was beautiful, peaceful and other worldly. Moving along the hard sand the ocean washed her feet and the tiny breathing holes of the beach dwellers popped and bubbled in the dimness.

She walked as far as the rocks and trudged up through the soft sand and found the rocky seat that was a favourite during the day. The boulders still held the heat of the sun and she shuffled backwards to rest against the warm hardness. It was slack tide and the waves were little more than silver frills on the edges of the great billow. She felt safe and calm and so very lucky to be here in this moment.

She closed her eyes. The darkness had never held any fear for her. She knew only too well that danger and trouble came in the full light of day and not from hidden mysteries but from the hands of those best known and closest. The murmur of waves lulled her mind and the dull rolling of the sea amongst the rocks sounded like the heartbeat of the very earth itself. If she were to sink down now and become one with the beach and the water and the wondrous sky she would have no regrets.

After a while a chill breeze rippled across the dunes and drew the tiny hairs on her arms to attention. She dragged on the warm sweatshirt that she had brought and with a sigh pushed herself up and began the walk back to the cottage and a cup of tea and the cosiness of the bright little lounge.

Should she come again tomorrow, or would familiarity spoil the magic? Well, the weather, her mood and instinct would inform her decision, but not the stories of ghosts in the sand dunes and hauntings on the cliffs.

She had felt no threat and no fear and had loved the whole experience.

As she trekked the last few yards to the little gate in the back garden there was the rumble of an engine. No light showed on the road and no swish of tyres gave witness to a passing vehicle. She paused beside the wall. A few hundred yards down the road a gleam in the hedgerow drew her attention. The moonlight glinted on a hard reflective surface – didn't it? Was a car parked in the gateway to the cow meadow? She couldn't be sure.

She closed the door behind her and went to the window to pull the drapes. The garden was shades and shadows save for the beautiful rambling rose. Tree branches shifted in the stiffening breeze and down against the wall of the barn. Where the farm and cottage shared space, a darker shadow formed and moved and was swallowed by the night. She gulped. All the time on the beach she had known not a moment of unease and here, back in the snug little house she felt a chill of fear. She snatched the curtains closed and turned on the lights and double checked the locks on the old oak doors. Her neck prickled and she needed the noise from the radio and the comfort of a blanket around her shoulders although she had no idea what she was afraid of.

Chapter 12

Later, in the darkened bedroom, Pauline replayed the evening. She relived the pleasure of the walk on the sands and then the strange finale which had left her unsettled and nervous.

Had there been someone in the dark garden? She just couldn't be sure. Certainly there was movement in the corner by the barn wall. It could have been a trick of the light, a cloud on the moon or just her imagination. There was the rumble of an engine though. Perhaps that was just the trawlers out on the water and the effect of echo and wind. There had been a glint of something from the field gate. The moon was tiny and surely the light so very faint that it couldn't reflect on anything. The street light could perhaps be coming though and yet the movement of the trees in the breeze had made it tricky to see properly. Was there something? Was it imagination?

She flipped over onto her side and dragged the duvet tightly around her shoulders. The house was secure. Although it was away from the village, it was hardly deserted. The farm was just a few hundred yards away. She had her new phone on the bedside table. She was safe and, in any case, why should there be someone in the garden or in the lane? It didn't make any sense and here she was spoiling the wonderful evening worrying about something that hadn't happened.

She closed her eyes and used a meditation technique to lull herself into sleep. She travelled in her mind to a desert island and walked the deserted beach and the real and present swoosh of the waves from across the meadow made the familiar, virtual journey very real. When she slept, she slept deeply with dreams of the beach and the water and a presence in the cove and when she woke in the bright morning she puzzled about who the figure had been standing on the cliff top watching her. Dream and reality had melded and blurred and it was fascinating.

"Hello – are you there?

"Morning, Dolly, come in, I've put the kettle on."

"Lovely. How are you today?"

"I'm fine thanks. I can't believe how quickly the time is going though. I realised today that this time next week I'll be packing up to leave. I'm going to miss it here."

"Aww that's nice to hear but you've got a lot of exciting things ahead."

"Yes, yes I have. I have had a wonderful time though and last night was so brilliant. I went down to the beach in the dark and walked on the sand and sat in the rocks. It was amazing, hey and no ghost!" As she made the light-hearted comment a knot of unease pulled at her and she turned away, unsure whether the moment showed in her face.

"Well that's good. It was a beautiful evening. Did your friend go with you?"

"Sorry?"

"Your friend, did he go with you? I hope you don't mind me mentioning this by the way. You have rented the cottage and it sleeps four of course and it's fine to have someone to come and stay but you do need to let me know when there are extra people in. It's all to do with the fire regulations."

"I'm sorry, Dolly – I have no idea what you're talking about!"

"Oh. Well that's odd. Mind I didn't see him myself. Jim told me about him."

"Who?"

"Okay, Jim said that when he went up to check on the beasts in the top field he saw a friend of yours in the garden. He waved and the bloke waved back and then just went and sat on the little bench. It didn't seem strange or suspicious and the chap didn't seem put out. Jim said it was just as if he was waiting for you."

"Are you okay, Pauline, you've gone very pale. Hey, here, sit down."

"Sorry, Dolly, sorry, just a dizzy spell. I'm fine really. I… I just need my breakfast. But I assure you, I haven't got a friend here and I'm not expecting anyone. It must just have been someone needing a sit down perhaps? Maybe it was someone local? Perhaps if you ask Jim again?"

"Yes, yes I will. Well how odd."

The chill that she felt was nothing to do with a change in the weather and Pauline breathed a sigh of relief as the other woman gathered up her things and left to work in the vegetable garden.

She sat in the chair by the window staring out at the little wooden bench. Who the hell had been sitting there while she was away? She knew no-one apart from Dolly and Jim and none of the people from her past had any idea where she was.

Did they?

Chapter 13

The barn wall formed part of the garden boundary. Beside the old stones the soil was damp and soft. Pauline peered down through the heather and rose bushes. She had to check, though she hoped there would be nothing to find. The shadow and movement had been imagination and a movement of the light, hadn't it? No, not that, for she could see them now: footprints unmistakable in the dark earth. Perhaps they had been there for a long time? She had never come over here before peering and poking about; why would she? The branches scraped at her arms and hands. As she knelt to look more closely she caught her cheek on a sharp thorn and hissed with shock.

"'Ave you lost somethin' there?"

"Oh, Jim!"

"Your face is bleedin'. You need to be careful rootlin' down amongst them roses."

"Yes, yes. I'd better go in and wash it."

"Did you find it?"

"Find what, sorry?"

"Whatever you were lookin' for. Did you find it?"

"Oh, I wasn't looking for anything." She pulled herself up short and then decided not to be embarrassed.

She would tell him what she was doing. She would explain even though he would likely think her fey and silly. Jim was a down-to-earth farmer, he would ridicule her worries. Of course he knew nothing of where the fear came from and why she was reacting the way that she was.

She took a deep breath. "I was looking to see if someone had been here, Jim."

"Here, in this corner?" His glance down at the disturbed flower bed told her more than his puzzled words.

"Yes, here in this corner. I thought that I saw someone in the garden last night, in the dark."

"Aye, well. You'd been down on the beach bain't ya."

"Yes, I went down to walk on the sands in the dark. Did Dolly tell you?"

"Aye, she did. Daft ideas folks get, no wonder you'm havin' fancies. Anyway, let me in there."

He didn't push her aside but the way that he muscled in left Pauline no option but to move back onto the grass. All she could see for a moment was his round behind sticking out from the foliage and she had to fight the urge to giggle in spite of her fears. He used the gnarly old stick that he carried to swipe aside the sharper branches and then moved backward wiping his dirty hands down the front of his trousers.

"Aye, somebody's been in there. 'T'weren't me; too big for my feet. 'T'weren't Dolly neither. That chap I saw yesterday, Dolly said it weren't a friend a yours, s'that right?"

"Yes… I mean no. No, I wasn't expecting anyone. Nobody at all."

"Well, it could'a been a rambler. Them buggers don't know how to keep to the paths 'alf the time. Find 'em in the field with the beasts, in the farmyard, on the meadow. They just think the whole bloody place is some sort of holiday camp. This though, this is far in the corner. I don't know what to make a'this."

Butterflies fluttered in her stomach and Pauline had to clasp her hands tightly to hide the shaking of her fingers. She couldn't think of anything to say to this wrinkly old man as he stood before her with his head tipped to one side, puzzlement on his weather-beaten face.

"Do you want me to call the officer?"

"The officer?"

"Aye, him from the village. Police officer. Mind what he can do I can't think. All he can do is look and that won't help."

"No, no I suppose not. What do you think I, erm, we should do?"

"I reckon all's we can do is to lock up them doors and close yer curtains." As he spoke he reached out a grubby hand and laid it on her arm. "Don't you fret my dear. I'm just a shout away."

She could tell from this unlikely behaviour that her distress was showing on her face and she turned away so that Jim wouldn't see the swim of tears in her eyes. He was coming at this from a very different place than she. It wasn't a mystery to him but little more than a minor case of trespass to be sighed over and forgotten. For Pauline, though, the fear went deep. It couldn't be possible could it that George had tracked her down? Surely he hadn't stalked her and stood in the garden watching? Yet if it was George, if he had come, then what would he do? She gulped back the panic.

"Thanks, Jim. I guess I'll just have to be careful with the locks and so on."

"Aye, perhaps I should think about burglar alarms for yon windows and doors. All more trouble though, all more fuss."

"You going off down the sands now?"

"I was going to walk on the cliff path."

"Aye, well you enjoy that. I reckon there's a storm comin' so you make the most of it while you can."

"Bye, Jim. Thanks again."

He turned without another word and raised a hand in a sketchy wave as he stomped back the way that he had come into his farmyard.

Pauline went back into the cottage and collected her bag and coat. She checked the windows and pulled the bolt across the back door. She could do no more and so would put it out of her mind.

George couldn't have found her and she wouldn't let him take her pleasure. He had taken so much already and she was moving on. The tears were close as she strode away and out onto the well-worn footpath. Clouds across the sun echoed the sadness that she couldn't deny despite her resolve.

Chapter 14

Rain crept in during the day so Pauline cut short her walk. For a while she stood at the cottage window staring out at the dripping foliage, feeling alone and sad for the first time since she had made her break. If she and George had children there would be someone to talk to now, someone she would have brought with her. Truthfully though, she had to acknowledge if they had had children then it would mean that more people would be hurt by what had happened. If they had children she would have been tied even more tightly to George. The thoughts whirled and scuttered in her mind, aimless meandering considerations that didn't cheer her but lowered her mood even more.

She gave her head a shake. She mustn't let herself get down, not now when it had all gone so well. Perhaps it was time to leave this lovely little place and get started on the French adventure. There was only slightly less than a week to go, though, and she did love the cottage and the beach, and it was impossible to know how long it would be before she had the chance for another holiday.

And then she knew what she had to do. Pulling on her oldest trainers and a waterproof jacket she went out into the rain. She lifted her face to the gentle wash and immediately her spirits soared. She would go down to the beach and get soaking wet, she would paddle at the edge of the ocean and let the wind and the weather soothe her as it had always done. Many days hiking with bruises on both her body and her soul had proved that fresh air and exercise could do just as much and more than pain killers and sitting around wishing and regretting.

The sandy path was running with water. Before she had reached the dunes, her trousers were soaked and her shoes covered in mud. She felt like a child, a naughty child out in the rain without permission. By now she was laughing with the joy of it and as the rain trickled down from her dripping hair she licked it away. She felt ridiculous and foolish and free.

The beach was deserted. Grey clouds rested on the pewter ocean and screaming gulls rode the wind, their white wings flashing against the lowering sky. This world was so different from the one of yesterday and yet in its own way just as wonderful. As she walked the problems and sadness lifted and blew away and her confidence returned. She would take it one step at a time, it had worked so far and surely the worst was over anyway.

She wondered what George had done. No doubt by now the house would be in disarray, her spotless kitchen unrecognisable. He would probably have someone in to clean and manage her old home and she was pleased to find that she didn't care at all. The place had been so very full of pain. She couldn't find it in herself to care what happened to the bricks and mortar or the goods and chattels that had been so much subterfuge and window dressing. All lies, valueless and dead.

She was opposite the cliff now. It would be too wet in the usual place but perhaps she could find some shelter and sit for a while and watch the rolling water and breathe great lungfuls of the rain-washed air. She clambered over the boulders sliding and slipping now and again but making her way into the formation. There was a part overhung by rocks and she was able to push into the small space and tuck herself into a crevice. It wasn't exactly comfortable but she could sit for just a little while and be at one with the weather and the wildness.

Visibility wasn't good but it was possible to see as far as the place where the path emerged from between the dunes. She sat with her back against the damp rock and let her eyes roam unfocused across the beach and the waves.

A movement drew her gaze and she raised her head and screwed up her eyes the better to make out the dark figure across the beach. It wasn't Dolly or Jim; it was far too tall for either of them. As she watched the man walked a little way forward and turned back and forth as if searching. Dark clothes whipped and slapped around him as he raised a hand to shield his eyes from the wet.

He didn't go down to the water's edge or turn and stride out along the sand. He had no dog that she could see. He was alone.

The rain was heavier now and she knew that she would have to move soon as she was soaked through. Although that had been part of the intention it would be irresponsible to stay too long in wet clothes with the cold rain trickling down her back. She could feel the chill and was already looking forward to a warm shower.

For the moment though something kept her in her tiny enclave. Some sixth sense hid her from the figure on the beach and as she watched he turned and climbed back up the dunes. He didn't use the path but struggled through the tall grass. He bent now and again on the steeper dunes using his hands to help him struggle upwards. He reached the old stone wall and with a final turn to the beach and a quick scan around him he threw one leg over, hoisted himself onto the top and dropped into her garden.

Her heart pounded. What on earth should she do? Did anyone have the right to walk into that land? But even if they did, then why approach from the beach? Why not use the gate? She pulled out her phone to call Dolly. Her fingers fluttered on the keys but at the last moment she clicked the off button and replaced the tiny handset in her pocket.

It wasn't George. She would have recognized him, surely, but had he sent someone? Had he found her? Yet how was it possible? She had been so very careful. Tears mingled with the rain running down across her face; tears of fear, shock and frustration. What on earth was she going to do now?

Chapter 15

Pauline pushed out from the dripping rocks. Instead of sliding and slithering down the streaming boulders, she searched for handholds to pull herself up the front of the small cliff face. She didn't want to be exposed on the beach.

Water streamed into her face and her nails broke and split as she scrabbled for safe places to cling on with the ends of her fingers. Her feet kicked and probed for footholds.

She pulled herself over the top and onto the sheep nibbled grass in the meadow. Scurrying to the sopping hedge she made her way down the edge of the field to the garden wall. She was able to crouch beneath it to make her way to the road. Mud sucked and pulled at her squelching shoes as the wind-blown rain slanted into her streaming eyes. The grey day had closed around her now and the delight of just a short while ago was lost in the desperate struggle of the moment.

There was no sign of a car parked on the verge or in the gateway to the field. Now that she was near to the little cottage she was unsure what to do next. The man from the beach wasn't visible in the garden but he could be round the other side of the building, in the front or indeed inside.

She slid through the front gateway and ran in a half crouch across the path to bob under the little front window. There was no noise that she could make out save the splosh and bubble of the rain in the gutters and drain pipes. She raised her head far enough to be able to peer into the lounge. All seemed undisturbed and empty. At a half run she covered the distance down the side of the house and through the tall gate into the back garden. There was no-one obviously there and she strode across the flagged patio to where it was possible to see into the kitchen, which was deserted and calm.

The bolt was fastened on the kitchen door so Pauline made her way to the front of the house. As she slipped the key into the lock the sound of an engine spun her around and from behind the bus stop two hundred yards up the road a dark car rolled out onto the road and drove past the cottage. She tried to peer inside but it sped past, picking up speed. It was just possible to make out was a dark clad figure behind the rain splattered windscreen. As it sped off into the misty distance she stepped inside and slammed the door behind her. Was it possible that this was someone sent by George? Would he really go to the lengths of hiring someone? It was a ludicrous thought. Ordinary people like her weren't followed by private detectives.

She slid to the floor and let out a sighing breath. What the heck was going on? Her nerves were jangled, her shoes and clothes were filthy and wet, and her soaking hair streamed into her eyes. Standing in the hallway she peeled off the sopping outfit and bundled it all together to throw into the kitchen. She would have a hot shower before she sorted out the laundry and stuffed her wet shoes with newspaper.

With the hot water pounding her skin and steam billowing around her she made a huge effort to regain control of her emotions and unscramble the events of the last couple of hours.

She was making a mountain out of a mole hill. A man walking on the beach, even in the rain, wasn't suspicious. Hadn't she done the very same thing herself? A man climbing over the garden wall wasn't innocent behaviour however, and a car hidden behind the bus shelter effectively on the pavement was decidedly odd. She would tell Dolly. There was very likely an innocent explanation. Probably it was someone they knew who used the garden as access. She must stop seeing danger everywhere she went.

Chapter 16

Clean and dressed in soft trousers and a sweatshirt, Pauline dried her hair and sprayed herself with perfume. Her agitated nerves had settled in the warm steam and pounding spray and as she made her way to the kitchen she felt her world had pretty much righted itself again.

There was still a puzzle to be solved but in reality it probably had nothing to do with her. No-one locally knew who she was and when she spoke to Dolly in the morning no doubt an explanation about the afternoon's upset would be found and if not, well so be it. She had come to no harm and now felt foolish imagining her desperate dash across the meadow and the ducking and diving behind walls and under hedges.

When her mind began replaying yet again the strange happenings she deliberately pushed them aside. There could be no solution found tonight and what she needed to do was put the worry away and try to have a pleasant evening.

She needed comfort food and she needed wine. Cheese on toast would hit the spot and the bottle of red she had opened the day before.

Once the food was ready she carried it through to the living room and turned on the table lamps and the jazz she had been listening to the night before. With a contented sigh she settled back on the sofa with a plate of bubbling cheese on toast and leaned over to place the glass on the side table.

The food was delicious, exactly what she needed after the upheaval of the day and she closed her eyes to enjoy the moment...

She leaned to put the empty plate beside her and her fingers found a small scrap of paper. She idly picked it up and unfolded it.

Gull's Rest
Porthelland
Jim and Dolly Teague
07864 342281 mobile

She folded the paper again and dropped it back where she had found it. Laying her head back she lost herself in the music.

The concern at the back of her mind grew slowly. She put down her glass and picked up the post-it note. Pink with a daisy in the top right hand corner. The same as the ones she had kept on her desk in the house in The Dales.

Her throat threatened to close. She hadn't put this paper here. Dolly had cleaned the room and there had been no bits and pieces left about. Both herself and the cottage owner were tidy and neat. She had used this table for her morning coffee cup and it was clean and empty.

She knew it was her paper and it was her writing – there was no doubt – but she certainly hadn't put it in this room.

Where had she last had it? She had been so very careful to keep all her information on her MacBook, the one that George didn't know she had, the one that stayed hidden in the old suitcase in the wardrobe.

She had written the address down just once. Sitting at her desk ready to leave and then thinking ahead to when she would arrive in Cornwall. She had scribbled it down at the last minute in case she needed to call.

She tried to calm herself. Just like the man in the garden this would have a simple explanation.

Closing her eyes, she replayed her departure and remembered. She had slipped this into her jacket pocket and as she began the walk had pushed her jacket into the bag: the jacket that she no longer had because it was lying in a ditch at the side of the road.

Wasn't it?

Chapter 17

She held the little square of paper in her hands, folding and unfolding it. It must be that she had brought it into this room and put it on the table. Or maybe, it had been on the floor and Dolly had picked it up and put it here for her to find. Yes, that's what had happened.

But it wasn't.

Pauline knew. This piece of paper had been in her jacket pocket. The ambulance people told her to keep the unconscious man in the ditch warm and sent her running for her bag and dragging out the jacket. She had wrapped it around his shoulders and chest and felt the shivering ease.

She had been so scared that he would die. It was frustrating that she didn't know what else to do but sit beside him and hold his hand, so then she had wrapped him in her coat.

So, had the paper fallen out into the road or into her bag? Maybe it had been in her bag and had become tangled in the other clothes. Yes, yes, then she hadn't noticed it when it fell out and Dolly had found it. That was it, that's what had happened.

Why then did it have a water stain in the corner and a strange brown smear across one side?

She screwed the thing up and took it with her into the kitchen. She didn't need it now and it wasn't important so it was dropped into the bin. The accident had been horrible. It wasn't something she wanted to think about, now or ever, but it would have been nice to know how he had fared, the broken and unconscious rider.

Why was it that every time she moved forward, something seemed to pop up to take her one step back and mar her pleasure? Damn it, the paper was nothing, just a strange little mystery and not worthy of a moment's thought.

She poured another glass of wine and settled back on the settee to lose herself in the rich sounds of saxophone and piano.

Too much wine, too much emotion, and it was time for bed. She checked the doors and dragged herself upstairs. Tomorrow was forecast to be bright and sunny so she would go to the beach and remind herself that she was supposed to be on holiday. Time was running out and she must make the most of these last few days.

The waxing moon peeped through the tree tops so she left the curtains open. The morning sun would waken her but that was fine as she wanted to fill her day with pleasure.

When the puzzles and memories tried to push in she cast them aside. She went on her mental journey to the desert island. Walking on white sand under swaying palms beside an azure ocean. The gentle rush of waves on the beach both real and virtual lulled her to sleep…

It was fear that woke her although it took a while to register. Music played somewhere softly in the darkness.

The moon washed the space with silver light. For a moment Pauline lay in the warm bed puzzled by the frizzle of nerves.

The smoky note of a saxophone drifted into the room.

As she slid her legs from under the duvet goose pimples prickled her bare arms. She realised that she was holding her breath and gave herself a moment to breathe and to listen and assess.

Slowly she crossed the carpet and reached a hand to the half-closed door. The music swelled and faded waves of it wafted up the stairs; enticing, puzzling and drawing her onwards in spite of herself.

She took the few steps across the landing and peered over the balustrade. The front door was closed, the living room door was open. There was the source of the sounds.

She gulped, her throat had dried and her stomach quivered with nerves. She looked back, it would be wisest to return to the safety of the bedroom, lock the door and ring the police on her mobile. Yet fear of embarrassment, a disinclination to cause a fuss, maybe even some curiosity; whatever it was something carried her quietly down the wooden staircase.

She crept along the hall and stood outside the lounge listening. The music still played, otherwise all was quiet save for the click of the hot water boiler which suddenly chimed in and caused her to gasp with shock.

She pushed open the door and stepped into the room. A figure sat in the easy chair by the window, backlit by the faint glow from the lamp in the farm gateway. A dark silhouette; his hands on the arms of the chair his feet planted flat on the floor. A shadow statue.

She took another step and his eyes opened and gleamed in the dimness. It wasn't Jim and despite what she had come to assume, this wasn't George either.

Chapter 18

Shaking fingers clutched at her pyjama top, knuckles gleaming bone white. Tears of fear and panic swam in her eyes as Pauline hissed at the figure. Her voice hitched and caught as she struggled for control. "I'm not going back. I don't care what he's said, what he's told you. I won't go back. You can't make me, he can't make me." She sobbed into the continuing silence.

For a long moment the dark shape didn't move, he simply sat four square in the armchair; then she saw his fingers stretch and flex. She backed away towards the door. She must run.

The voice stopped her. "Sit down. Sit down now."

"I've called the police. They'll be here any minute." In response to her desperate lie the man simply raised his hand and turned her little phone in his fingers. He pressed the button causing the tiny screen to light up and shook his head. He had been into her bedroom while she slept. He had stepped beside her bed and taken the phone from her cabinet.

She couldn't breathe.

"No, you didn't. Sit down there." He pointed to the settee. She wouldn't sit, wouldn't be ordered around. Never again, she had left all that behind.

"No. Get out. Tell him that I am not coming back no matter what and tell him to leave me alone."

He moved too quickly. Out of the chair, across the room. He reached the corner where she was backing into the hall. He leaned behind her and slammed the heavy wooden door, and in the same move grabbed her arm and dragged her to the settee. He half threw, half pushed her into the soft cushions.

A deep pain in her upper arm begged for relief. She rubbed at it as she drew her legs up, curling defensively in the corner of the seat. "Please, don't hurt me. There's no need for you to hurt me. I don't know what he told you but he's a brute and a bully. I had to get away. Whatever he paid you I'll give you double. Just leave me alone and tell him you couldn't find me. Please, please!" The begging faded to a whimper as the tall man stood looking down at her. It was too dark to see his expression but his stance, the clenched fists and bunched shoulders quieted her.

"Right. That's better. Now listen to me. I will go away and you'll never see me again. I will leave you alone and I won't hurt you. All you have to do is give me them."

Pauline shook her head. "I don't know what you mean. I haven't got anything. I left everything. He can have it all I don't want anything more than I have here. I didn't take anything. I'm going to France..." The feeble final, desperate sentence died on her lips.

He held out his hand palm upward as if to receive some gift. "Give me them now and I will go. This can be over very quickly. Now I know you're a clever girl. Very clever. In fact, I'm impressed." He gave a short nod. "I am very impressed you covered your tracks so well and you didn't have a lot of time. A quick thinker, I like that and because I am so impressed I'm willing to finish this quickly. Now stop snivelling and just give me what's mine."

"I… what's yours? I don't know what you mean!" She was shaking her head, tears streamed down her face. She wiped her nose on the back of her hand and choked on a sob. She was terrified and out of her depth.

He crouched in front of her. One hand on the arm of the settee and the other on the seat close to her leg. She could feel his breath on her face and see the glimmer of moisture in his eyes. He leaned even closer as she pushed herself back into the cushions.

"I am trying to make this easy for you girl. I've had quite a time finding you. Giving the police a fake phone number and a duff address was all very clever. Thinking on your feet, but it didn't work. Oh, they gave them to me alright when I begged." He adopted a high pitched whining tone. "Oh, officer you must tell me who she is. She's my guardian angel! You must let me talk to her, I have to thank her. I want to send flowers and give her back her jacket. But then in the end it didn't matter because you had left me that nice little note in your pocket, hadn't you?" Pauline drew in a gasp of air.

"George didn't send you?" The frown that ran across his forehead answered the question as clearly as any words. "Who are you?" Of course she knew who he was but none of it made any sense. If he was the motor cyclist, then why was he angry? "You're the man from the road, aren't you? The accident. I thought you were in hospital."

"Oh, I was for a few days. A nasty concussion and some knocks and bangs but they soon threw me out."

"The newspaper said you were seriously ill. I thought you might die."

"Yes, well sorry but here I am large as life and twice as ugly, so now you need to just do as I say."

"But, I don't understand you."

"Oh yes, I think you understand me very well indeed. You thought you could hide away, didn't you? But you're an amateur. I'm one of the best and if we don't settle this soon you'll rue the day you decided to try and fool me." He leaned and gripped her face in his big fingers squeezing till she felt warm blood in her mouth from where teeth punctured the inside of her cheeks.

"Now, okay, you made a good run for it – well done but it's over. I need my stuff back and I need it now. There are people waiting for the delivery and believe me they are not people you want to meet. Now it's up to you; easy or hard." With a rough gesture he flung her head away from him and stretched again to his full height towering over where she curled whimpering in the dark.

"I haven't got anything! Truly I haven't!"

"You went through my pockets. I know you did."

"Well I did, yes. I needed your phone, to call for help. I didn't have mine."

"Yes, but my other pockets; you went through my other pockets and you lifted what you found there didn't you? I bet you thought it was Christmas. Oh, you thought, I can have a little trip to Cornwall, and then what? Oh yes, France! You thought you'd just pop across the channel. Well, I don't think so, Pauline. I don't think so at all."

"Well, yes. I'm going to France, I am. But it was all planned already, before I left home. I was leaving home."

"Right, you were leaving home and going to France and just on the way having a stroll through The Dales and a trip to Cornwall."

"No, no, it isn't like that… well yes, I suppose it is, but..." She drew in a shuddering breath. "I was leaving my husband and I found you. I tried to help you. I didn't take anything."

"Right, let's just give him a call."

"What?"

"Your husband. Let's you and me give him a little call, see if he's missed you. Do you think he has, this mystery husband? Do you think he's missed his Pauline?"

"No, no you can't you mustn't! He can't know where I am! He'll come and find me! Oh please, don't do this."

"Give me the bag you took from my pocket and I'll leave you. I have to tell you though I am feeling a bit impatient now. You're pushing me and you don't want to do that."

"I haven't got anything. I didn't take anything."

"Oh dear. I see you don't really understand what you've got yourself into here. Those diamonds didn't belong to me. That memory stick is important to my clients. They don't want it falling into the wrong hands and you – well I'm afraid you are the wrong hands."

"Diamonds? Memory stick? I haven't got any diamonds."

"Oh, come on now, that won't wash. This is not going to end well for you if you insist on playing the innocent."

Then with an alarming burst of speed he leaned down and grabbed Pauline and hoisted her to her feet. He pulled both arms up behind her back and she screamed as hot flashes of pain seared her muscles.

"Don't! please! please don't..."

"You can stop this right now but I'm warning you, I am not a patient man." With the words of threat ringing in her ears the darkness came and took her as she sagged forward in his grasp.

Chapter 19

Someone was crying. As she fought her way to the surface, Pauline clamped down on the pitiful sobs.

Panic overwhelmed her, she couldn't move, couldn't see and she hurt, badly, everywhere. As reality dragged her back from the dark, each and every pain became more acute.

Inside her mouth was raw, her arms screamed, her legs were a deep ache. Her thumbs were searing ice. Her stomach roiled and acid burned in her throat. She retched but managed to hold back the nausea. A hard-edged leather strap gagged her mouth and made swallowing almost impossible. Drool slipped sickeningly across her cheek. Every movement was torment. She had suffered pain before, often, but this was on a different level to that which she had become accustomed to at the hands of her husband.

It puzzled her that she was still in the little cottage. On the floor in the living room, in the dark. Her hands were awkward lumps beneath her and it was impossible to separate them. Her thumbs screamed their objection when she tried.

She tried to swivel her head around to see him, to find where he was, but even this small movement caused such agony that she soon gave up. She couldn't sense his presence in the room. Hope bloomed; maybe he had gone? He had immobilised her in the most cruel way. Although she wasn't actually fastened down, something was around her thumbs and her big toes were tied together with a stiff narrow band cutting off the circulation and preventing any attempt to stand. Her legs were pulled into an unnatural bow, her ankles twisted. Every movement shot lightning bolts through her entire body. The music still played, the gentle sound of jazz, smooth and liquid, mocked this nightmare she had woken to.

She felt the bump through the old building. He was still here then, upstairs perhaps, or in the kitchen. Footsteps across the ceiling answered the question. He was thumping and banging in the bedroom. Searching for things she didn't have.

Her frame shook and juddered though she tried to ease the effect of the shivering on the damaged parts of her body. Her world was a flood of pain, and despair swept in to overwhelm her. She didn't think she wanted to live now. She wanted to be away from this, to fall back into the recent darkness and float away. Nobody could stand this, yet she shivered and breathed and cried salt tears which dribbled across her face and stung her ruined lips and the peace refused to take her back.

The thud of feet on the stairs told her he was coming back. She closed her eyes and tried to still the shivering. It was impossible, her body was crying out for ease and could find it nowhere.

He nudged her with the toe of his boot. "You awake now?" She screwed her eyes tight. "Aha, I see you are. Well now, we have a problem, don't we?" He crouched beside her and with the ball of his thumb prised open one eyelid. "Come on now, wakey wakey. You need to talk to me, Pauline.

"Are you going to be sensible now and tell me where you've hidden them? Oh, I do hope you haven't sold them. That would be a very bad situation indeed. He grabbed her face and forced her to look at him. "You haven't sold my pretty diamonds, have you?"

She shook her head.

"Good, well that's good. So, all you need to do now is tell me where you've put them and where you have my memory stick and then we can all be on our way."

She shook her head again, trying to make him believe her innocence, but he scowled at her and squeezed tightly with his fingers. She gasped with the fresh pain. "Oh, now come on. You have to see this is really not going to work." She shook her head desperately from side to side. He had to understand she couldn't give him what she hadn't got.

"Oh dear." He straightened and then bent from the waist and in a moment of exquisite agony she was dragged to her feet and pulled to the sofa where he threw her into a slouch and then knelt before her.

"You will tell me. I can't understand why you don't see that. You have taken what was mine and I want it back. It's simple and now you have made me very angry." He snorted, great shoulders shrugging with the expiration of air.

* * *

An incongruous blackbird threw a song to the new morning. As the answering bird call tinkled in the garden he walked through to the hallway and came back with her coat and bag.

"Right, I have to go now." A blessed relief swept her body. "But, I can't leave you here, can I? You do see that? I can't have you talking to people and I need you to tell me where my property is. This is not over; I don't want you to think this is over. I am not going to just walk away; I can't. You think this is bad, Pauline? Well let me tell you that if my clients get their hands on you you'll wish for me to come back.

"Now, I have told them I have this all under control, and I do. I do because one way or the other you are going to tell me what I need to know. So, what am I going to do with you now while I go and take care of business?

"Well I have a treat for you. You like to go and walk on the beach don't you, Pauline? Yes you do, I've seen you. Well we're going on the beach now. You and me are going down to the seaside before anyone else is up and about and we're going to find a nice quiet place for you to spend the day. You'd like that wouldn't you, a nice day on the beach? Well, I say on the beach! Ha."

Her panicked eyes flicked from side to side as he collected her coat and phone and bag, and then dragged her upright. He bent and snipped open the cable ties on her toes; the pain as circulation flooded the numbed digits with blood took the strength from her knees. He held her upright with an arm around her waist and forced her forward and out of the room. Through the back door they shuffled in an obscene waltz and then he dragged her across the little lawn and out onto the meadow. Staggering painfully across the wet grass she prayed for oblivion as the gulls wheeled and screamed and the sunrise painted golden sequins across the water.

Chapter 20

Cool sand under her feet; a precious bead of relief in the pool of pain.

He had dragged her beside him, scuttling and tripping over rough grass, down the grit of the dunes and now he marched in the damp hardness of the tide-washed beach. Her hands were still fastened behind her and she leaned forward for balance, stumbling when he forced her onward too quickly.

Breath burned in her throat and a stitch caught at her side. Her jaw was a persistent ache and as she tried to swallow, her damaged tongue caught on the hard gag. Everywhere was pain and it melded until all there was in the whole world was agony and evil. No nightmare had ever been so vile; no imagined scenario under the hammer of George's control had come close to this and she couldn't see how she would ever bear it.

Now they reached the rocks. Surely he wouldn't make her climb, not with her hands tied and her feet bare, but he did. He pushed her on before him and steadied her with two hands, one on each arm. Sometimes he missed his footing and dragged on her screaming limbs and she groaned into the early daylight as tears tracked across her wounded face.

When they had climbed six feet or maybe a little more above the beach he dragged her to a halt and leaned to hiss into her ear. "I'm taking the tie off. Don't even think of trying to run." White heat seared her hands and as her arms dropped to her sides the fire in her shoulders caused her eyes to flood with fresh tears and stole her breath away. He forced her to her knees on the wet rocks.

He stepped now to the front and dragged a piece of rope from his jacket. Ignoring her gasps and groans he pulled her wounded arms forward and tied them loosely by the wrists. Fisting his hands in her hair he dragged her back to her feet and drove her on and up. The cliff was steeper now. This was higher than she had been before, though she had clambered to the sheep field from the lower levels closer inland. As they climbed they headed southwards out onto the rocky promontory. Would he drown her then? Would she be dashed to a pulp on the Cornish coast and become another statistic in the annals of foolish walkers and irresponsible tourists? So be it; she would have peace at least. Her feet were soled with blood and grit where sharp stones had stabbed and torn. Stumbling and slithering they made their way until at the start of the descent he turned and pushed her to his left.

There was a fissure in the rock. How had he found this place? Of course, the stranger in the garden, at the fete and on the beach had been him, watching and exploring and planning and it had come to this. The floor sloped downwards inside the cliff where a small cave had been formed by centuries of rushing tides. So then, this was where she would die. He pushed her onto a narrow ledge and she curled forward and hid her face in bleeding hands and sobbed.

"I didn't want to do this, Pauline. You have brought this on yourself. You do see that don't you?" He dragged on a handful of hair forcing her to face him "I said, you do see don't you that this is all your fault?"

She couldn't speak but just stared up at him in the mild light and was subsumed by hopelessness.

"All you have to do is to tell me where you've put the stuff. That's all." In truth he seemed anguished and she realised then that fear had some part in what was driving his viciousness. If she could have given him anything at that moment, anything in the world to stop this, then she would. She could not though, for she had nothing he wanted.

He leaned and untied the belt from around her face. The pain in her jaw was expected now, coming as it did after so much; so she gingerly closed her mouth and felt the roil of nausea and rode it and breathed through it.

"Why won't you tell me?"

She shook her head. It was hard to form the words but a whisper came and found its way through her swollen lips. "I can't. I haven't got them. Haven't got anything. Never had anything."

He spun away from her with a curse and kicked at the ground. "Right, right. You'll stay here now and, if the sea doesn't get you perhaps you'll see sense." She gave a small shake of her head; she was done.

He made her stand again and pushed her further into the darkness along the ledge, pressed against the rock wall. He grabbed her hands and tied them behind her and then ran the rope down and round her feet. He dragged the belt from his pocket but after peering at the wounds in the corners of her mouth he growled at her. "There will be no use shouting; nobody will hear you. Nobody comes here. I've watched and I've been down here and the waves are too loud so don't even bother calling out."

He turned and with no further backward glance scrambled into the light and left her alone with the roar of the ocean and the drip of salt water and the enormity of fear.

Chapter 21

When she was sure he was gone, Pauline screamed out. The effort tore at her throat and the sound was that of a desperate animal but she continued to yell until pain and exhaustion reduced the cries to a whimpering plea. "Oh please, please, someone. Please."

He had told her there was no point. He said the cave was too far from the quiet beach and the roar of waves would be too loud but she had needed to try.

There were no more tears left for her to cry now and her nerves were numbed. How was it possible that she was tied with rope in a dark, damp cave? She was Pauline Green. An ordinary person; she was just Pauline. The hard wetness of her perch and the constant drip of moisture argued for truth and in the end all she was able to do was mourn and wonder how it had come to this.

She shuffled and tried to ease the pain in her arms and shoulders, in her back and her neck. After a time she managed to swing her legs round and lay like a trussed chicken on the wet ledge. Shivers came in painful waves and with each one she whimpered through chattering teeth. There were no beach cries, no laughing children or barking dogs. The only sound was the sea, relentless, endless and timeless. It was hell, but then her body and her brain took her away from it. The oblivion that lulled her wasn't sleep but it was better than reality.

A variation in the noise brought her back to wakefulness, a rattle that wasn't there before. There was a rolling clatter that swelled with each wave.

The tide was coming in.

She wanted to sit up and look down into the depths of the cavern but it was beyond her. Lying on the hard stone her limbs and muscles had stiffened and she simply didn't have the strength in mind or body to fight the pain. She lay quietly, barely breathing.

How high would the water rise?

During the last hours death had seemed a tempting thought, but now it was inconceivable that she should simply lie and wait for it. No matter how bitter, life is sweet and the least she must do was to try to survive. She gritted her teeth and with a bark of pain managed to swing her legs around. After almost toppling from the ledge she desperately shuffled her behind backwards and dragged her feet up. Now that her knees were bent the pull on her arms was eased. Spots of sunshine shone through holes in the rocks above her and lit the wall in tiny smears of gold and she was able to peer down into the void.

Swirls of light and dark rushed to and fro across the bottom of the cave. Small boulders and pebbles rolled and played in the waves and filled the air with another layer of sound. The echo of the sea amongst the cliffs was louder now and she realised that when it was no longer possible to hear the pebbles it would be because they were submerged beneath the water. There was no weed inside where she was and she didn't know whether that was because of the lack of light or because the tide would fill the space, scouring it clean and snuffing out what was left of her. Terror rippled through her, she didn't want to drown there in the dark. Tears tracked down her face and a great sob sounded out into the void.

Near to her head was a tiny hollow in the dark wall and she shuffled closer. Leaning against the surface of the rock she slid her face towards the indentation and stuck out her tongue. She tasted sweet water. The relief was overwhelming. It was rainwater seepage from the rocks above. So, did this mean that she would not drown? If the water were not salt then surely it was because the tide didn't reach this far. It must do, surely. With agonising slowness she leaned lower until her lips touched the cold puddle and she sucked the gritty nectar into her damaged mouth; although it was only enough to wet her lips and tongue, it was bliss. She shuffled further along the ledge, yes, another dip, another small drink and then another. In her excitement she almost toppled into the depths and she stopped and took some deep breaths to calm herself. In the depths of despair and fear she was amazed to feel the stretch of a smile on her face. A small victory, a tiny triumph and as she licked the walls of her prison she found a new resolve to endure.

No-one would search for her. He had taken her coat and bag and hidden them in the dunes and so when Dolly came for their morning coffee she would assume that she had gone for a walk. He had made no obvious mess in the house it didn't seem, so there was nothing to raise the alarm. He would return though; when he had done whatever had taken him away today he would come back and berate her again and bully and try to make her confess. She must find a way to convince him that she had no diamonds and no computer memory stick. But then, like a dark worm, the thought uncoiled: what would he do when he realised that she was, in truth, of no use to him at all?

Chapter 22

To drive back the terror, Pauline had to hold onto a belief in her future. If she accepted that death was inevitable then surely the best and quickest thing to do was to throw herself from the ledge to drown in the swirling water. But no; this wasn't an option. She knew that she would relive this horrible event for the rest of her life, supposing there was to be more life for her. If, when she thought of it, she saw herself as a snivelling coward, then it would torment her, so she resolved to endure and tried to think; to plan.

The rainwater soothed her mouth and throat. The dripping soothed her nerves because while there was dripping she would be able to drink. Each little pool and hollow filled quickly and she blessed the inclement weather of the last few days.

Her wrists were raw, the skin torn and enflamed with rope burns. She pulled and twisted at the ties but it had only brought more pain. She had coiled and stretched her aching limbs every way that she could in an attempt to loosen the rope around her ankles, but in her confined position on the ledge and with the insults already paid to her body she had to acknowledge finally that she couldn't escape the bonds.

In books and films there would be sharpness in the rocks. She would saw the ropes until the strands gave way and she would be free. But the place that she was in had been smoothed by eons of tides. The rocks were rounded. She had shuffled back and forth along the ridge but had found nothing rough enough. It was difficult to find a position where the rope was taut and she could still move. Nevertheless, endless minutes had been spent simply rubbing the rope along the edges of the rock, surely it would wear through. Rock, rope, hope; a desperate triumvirate. Yet rope held.

The gold smudges of sunlight moved across the walls. Pauline watched with exhausted eyes as the day rolled around. No-one found her and though there would be families and couples on the beach they were a lifetime away.

When he came, he came quietly and suddenly. An alteration in the atmosphere told her that she was no longer alone. For a breathless moment she hoped for salvation but in the event it was the return of horror.

He had brought a torch this time and she was blinded as the beam flashed onto her face.

"Still here then?" He gave a short grunt of a laugh as he clambered up beside her.

There was no answer for her to make so she gave none. She had glanced at him once but now turned her face away.

"Well, Pauline." He sat in the damp with his legs swinging out into nothingness. Tiny scraps of rock and shutters of sand cascaded into the water of a slack tide. She stored the information away: he had come now, so even when the tide was high there was a way onto the promontory. He leaned towards her and murmured as to a friend in the cinema. A private *tête à tête* in the darkness.

"I popped back to the house. I haven't found my bag yet. You hid it well; I'll give you that. Then I got to thinking. Ah yes, I thought, I know what she's done, my friend Pauline. She's stashed it away from here."

She shook her head once.

"Anyway, no matter. I've been to see my clients again. Now to say that they are not happy doesn't even begin to cover it. They are very, very cross. Uh-huh." His head bounced up and down, a comedy routine, bizarre and terrifying. "Trouble is you see, they are cross with you. Well I'm cross with you as well, aren't I? The bigger problem though, Pauline, is that they are not happy with me and that is not what we want. When these people are disturbed it can end badly and one thing I can tell you is that I'm not going to let that happen to me.

"So, what are we going to do?"

Her hopeless monologue murmured through the darkening cave: "I haven't got anything. I truly haven't. Don't you think that if I did I would tell you by now? I don't know what you are talking about. I found you by the side of the road, I tried to help you. I didn't take anything. I lied about who I was because I didn't want my husband to find me."

"Well now that really does give us a problem doesn't it? Somebody has my stuff. Now who was there? Oh yes, there was you and… ah you see: there was just you." He twisted towards her and grabbed her face and she yelped in surprise and pain. "I will give you one last chance. You tell me where the stuff is hidden or you will never get out of this cave. Do you understand?" She nodded mutely, tears streamed down her face.

"Oh yes, and in case you were hoping for your landlady to come and look for you, I have sent a nice little text telling her how you have just met a friend and won't be back tonight. So, you don't need to have any concerns about them worrying. Thoughtful sort of chap, aren't I?"

She didn't see his hand rise but as he swiped backhanded across her face the world turned red and she thought that it was over. Yet in truth it was simply another beginning.

Chapter 23

He wasn't beating her because he thought it would elicit information. He must know by now that it wouldn't work. As he slapped at her face she knew he was beating her because, like George, it was his way to deal with frustration and fear.

Then the words popped out of her mouth almost before she thought them. "I buried it." Time held for a long moment. His head tipped to one side, his hand stilled in mid-air.

"What? What did you say?"

"I buried it. Your bag, I took it and buried it. I didn't know how to get rid of the stuff so I buried it until I had worked it out."

He turned away from her, confusion creased his brow. "Why, would you do this? Why would you let me bring you here? What, are you stupid or what? Why didn't you tell me?"

"I don't know."

"You better be telling me the truth. Are you lying to me?"

She simply shook her head and casting her eyes downwards, she sighed.

"Where did you bury them?"

"Under a rock on the cliff walk."

"Where? Which rock?"

"I… I don't know how to describe it. It's about half an hour in… there are some fallen rocks. It's overlooking a bay. I picked a rock that I thought I'd remember and I dug a hole under it."

Her mind was racing now. She tamped down the thrill of hope that flickered in her gut. She must keep calm.

"You'll have to take me. You'd better not be lying." He paced to the cavern entrance. It was too much to hope that he would take her onto the beach while people were still there but it was early evening now. Maybe soon he would risk it. Take her while there was still light in the day. She had to bend this tiny straw of possibility her way.

"I don't think I'll be able to find it in the dark. I'll show you tomorrow."

"What? What did you say? Who the hell do you think you are to start dictating terms? You'll show me when I say you will! You'll show me today."

He climbed back to sit beside her and dragged a bottle of water from his pocket. He lifted it to his lips and drank deeply. She held her breath; surely he would give her a drink. He must know how she needed one. Her desperate eyes watched as the water glugged and bubbled and his throat worked swallowing the cool liquid. Without a glance at her he finished the contents and then dropped the empty plastic bottle into the swirling depths. She felt hate then; more than she had ever felt in her life. More than for George and his brutality and more than even for this man up until now. It lit a fire deep inside that she feared would consume her and tip her over the edge into insanity. She clenched her fist and felt the pain in her fingers as she held back the fury.

Pauline was exhausted. Every bone and muscle ached with a deep throbbing relentlessness. Her eyes were sore, her throat was dry, she wasn't able to reach her pools and her head pounded. The brute sat beside her silent and calm.

"Who are you?"

"What?"

"Your name, what's your name?"

"What the hell has that got to do with you?"

"Nothing, sorry nothing. I just thought that… I don't know your name."

"You don't need to know my name. You don't need to know anything about me. All you need to be thinking about now is where that bloody rock is and what I might do to you if you're lying to me. So shut up."

She felt his tension, "Have you got any water?"

"No, No I haven't got any bloody water, you just saw me finish the water. Now – shut up."

How far could she safely go? She needed to needle him to the extent that he would act but not so much that he would lash out again. She couldn't take any more pain.

"Can I sip from that little hollow? That's what I was doing."

"Oh, bloody hell. Can't you shut up?" He clambered to his feet. She held her breath as he scrambled to the entrance. *"Please, please, please."* Silently pleading she was tight with tension.

"Right, come on. Now listen to me. I can put the gag back in or you can promise me that you won't shout or scream. Your choice but I'll tell you this, you try and draw attention to us and you will think that what has happened up to now has been a church picnic. I can think of ways to hurt you that you can't even begin to imagine. Do you understand?"

She nodded.

He bent and began to untie the rope around her ankles. Every nerve was a red hot needle. There might just be one chance and if there was she must grasp it. She must risk it all now because once he found that she had lied and that there was no bag, she was sure that he would not let her live.

Chapter 24

He unwound the rope from her feet and in a flood of pain her arms were pulled from behind her back.

"Christ, oh good Christ." Blackness hovered at the edges of the world and she bit the inside of a cheek to force herself to focus and cling to consciousness.

He tied the rope again around her wrists and cut off the excess, dropping it to the bottom of the cave. His merciless fingers lifted her head. Tears filled her eyes and as she blinked them away they dribbled across his hand.

"Bloody hell. Bloody snivelling women." He dashed the moisture on the legs of his jeans.

"Listen to me now, bitch. We are going to walk up the cliff. I've left the rope loose so you can balance. See how kind I can be when you co-operate? But if you make any silly moves, if you try to attract attention, if you do anything that annoys me you are going over the edge. Do you understand?"

Pauline sniffed and nodded. Holding the trailing edge, he led her forward. Though she was stiff and sore the long miles of hiking had made her strong. Her muscles remembered how to flex and stretch and on quivering legs she staggered towards the fading light at the cave entrance.

He pushed before her and gesturing with a hand behind him to keep her back, he moved on to climb the first of the rocks. He turned towards the beach and watched for maybe a minute, perhaps more. When he was satisfied he tugged on the rope. She followed like a tethered beast.

For the first part of the climb she concentrated on finding her footing. As her joints loosened and warmed her movements became more fluid, stronger with each step. He was two paces ahead and confident in his ability to clamber on the wet cliff. She watched, assessed, waited.

She tripped, tugged on the rope and he turned back with a snarl. "Bloody well take care, bitch, you'll have us over!"

"Sorry." She kept her head down, her gaze averted. She tripped again and came down on her knees."

"Shit! Will you stop?" He turned and stepped back half a pace.

"I'm sorry, I'm stiff and sore. My legs won't work properly."

"Stop whining." With a shake of his head and a sigh he leaned and tugged at the binds around her wrists and then he hooked a hand under her elbow and hoisted her upright. "There, now come on."

She wobbled on the next step and fell again; this time fully across the rocks. The rope tightened and he spun round in alarm. "Bloody hell! Can't you be careful?"

She lay full length and began to sob. He slithered towards where she was with her head on the rock and her leg between two great boulders.

"I'm trapped. I don't think I can move. Please, help me. My leg's stuck."

He threw the rope aside in fury and stepped across her.

As he bent to the rocks she closed her eyes and drew up her knees. With all the strength left in her battered body she kicked out at him. Both feet connected with his lower belly and he tumbled back amongst the loose stones at the edge of the promontory.

"Shit!"

Pauline curled forward and threw herself at him. She screamed with the effort and felt him grab at her hands, pawing at her arms in panic. The ground beneath him was unstable and rocks and pebbles cascaded into the swirling water. She shook him off and fell back onto her behind. Drawing up her knees again she planted both feet flat against his chest and with a mighty kick pushed him further over the brink.

"Bitch! Bitch!" He screamed at her, but he was clawing now at the crumbling edges and she kicked again and again beating down on him with her heels and thrusting with all the strength left in her legs. She heard the crack as his nose broke under the onslaught of her pounding feet and then with a rumble of rock and a final screech from him, the verge collapsed and carried him away into the tumbling waves.

He screamed again.

She heard the thud of him bounce against the rocks.

Then there was nothing but the cry of the gulls and the waves breaking on the shore.

She couldn't move. She simply lay on the rocks for now and just breathed but knew that she would have to look.

On hands and knees, she crawled forward. Then, stretched full length again, because she suspected that her legs wouldn't hold her, she peered over the edge. His body was far below. She couldn't tell if he was alive. He made no effort to swim and as the water took him towards the rocks she believed that at the very least he was unconscious.

She was still bound but able to push to her feet and clamber to the beach side of the rocks. Far below, walking in the evening light was a group of teens, a dog walker. She yelled to them and held up her arms. The nearest group turned and peered towards her. She lowered her aching arms; they would come now. She tried to shout but all that she could manage was a keening wail and then two of them turned and began to run away. As they did the sounds of their panicked calls floated back to her. They pointed as they went and then the others joined the dash; they ran from her, they ran from the creature in the rocks, they ran from the fabled figure on the headland, the ghoul from the past.

Hysteria took her now and she began to laugh as the tears rolled down her filthy face and the effort and the anguish took the strength from her legs and she flopped to the ground and lowered her head into her hands. If he had been alive, surely he was dead by now. She couldn't help him. She couldn't help herself, all she could do was to sit in the sunset and cry.

At last the world wheeled away and darkness descended. She was done, there was nothing left. It was over.

Chapter 25

The cold forced her back to the world; the cold and the shivering. When Pauline opened her eyes the sky above was indigo, and silver stars were sliding through the blanket so she knew she had been out of it for a while.

The pain in various parts of her body had become an old enemy by now, so pushing herself to a sitting position brought no surprises. The world tipped and swam but righted quickly and the slight nausea passed leaving her feeling drained.

The horror of the fight swarmed back in. She lowered her head and forced herself to breathe deeply. Was he still there? Was the body still swilling back and forth at the foot of the cliffs? Of course she would need to go and look.

She had killed a man.

What was she going to do now?

This wasn't something that could be fixed. He was dead. Wasn't he? Her mind's eye recalled the image of his body, arms flailing as he rolled towards the rocks.

It was her fault he was dead. How would she ever be able to bear it? Right now most of what she felt was empty. The fear was gone, the horror numbed by a sort of disconnection.

First, she had to get rid of the rope which was still around her swollen wrists. He had loosened it when she tripped repeatedly, so, with a little effort she was able to wriggle her hands free. She tossed it to one side among the boulders.

She leaned sideways and then rolled to her knees and, using the rocks for aid, managed to push herself upright. Stiffly she made her way to the edge of the cliffs and made herself look. His body was still caught in the tumble of rocks at the base of the promontory and the receding tide raised his arm and waved a hand to her. Surely it was just the action of the water? Could she be sure? Maybe he was still alive? Horror consumed her and bile rose in her throat.

She must clamber down. She should at least do that. She ran, small uncertain steps back and forth looking for a safe place but there was none. Often, she glanced back to where he lay. Whitewater broke against the body. Surely he must be dead. But did he not try just now to raise his head?

"Hello? Hello, can you hear me?" The only response to her desperate call was the roll of waves and the distant cry of a single gull making for his roost.

She didn't want to be responsible for the death of anyone. It was unthinkable! More tears, yet more, and she wiped them away on the back of her hand and admitted to herself it wasn't possible to reach him and that he was beyond help.

"I'm sorry, I'm so sorry but you hurt me. I wish you hadn't hurt me!" Leaving the whispered words to fade into the breeze she turned and staggered back towards the beach. She slipped and scrambled down the rocky side, opening old wounds and rubbing fresh grazes onto her hands and arm. But she felt none of it, for her soul was broken, her feelings were dead.

Was it possible that it had been just one day since he had forced her along the beach? Had driven her terrified and shaking and with no idea of the horror that she would endure and the tragedy that would unfold? She trudged past the road and to the dunes where he had hidden her bag and coat under some fallen pine branches. It was no surprise to find that they had gone. No great loss; a cheap phone, a few pounds in her change purse. It didn't matter.

At the cottage the little gate was ajar and she pushed through and up the sandy path to the kitchen door and there she stopped. What was she thinking? She must go to the farm, call the police, tell someone what had happened.

Could she bear it?

If she didn't, what then? There was another option: just leave the body to be found by a passing fisherman or an unsuspecting dog walker. Could she expunge this event from her history and pretend it had never happened? If she called the police they would question her and dig into her past. Perhaps they would find her account of the events as unbelievable as the motorcyclist had done? There were two distinct paths, one – the hardest – was to get help and face the consequences. The other was to run again, to fly from the terrible day and lock it away in the back of her mind and live with it.

She raised her hand to the door and realised that she had no key. If it was locked then she would have to go to Dolly and ask to be given access. Perhaps the choice wasn't to be hers to make after all.

Chapter 26

"Dolly, I'm sorry to disturb you but I've lost my key."

"Oh, good heavens, Pauline! What's happened?" Dolly stretched out her arms in automatic response to the figure standing in front of her. Then she hesitated; the other woman looked so damaged that she didn't know where it would be possible to touch without causing harm.

"I'm fine." Pauline tried to smile as the lie left her lips. "It's just that I've lost my key and I really need to get into the house. I'm sorry… I'll pay for the locks to be replaced."

"Locks? What are you talking about? What's happened? Come in for Pete's sake! Come in. Can you manage? Have you been in an accident? Oh no, you haven't been mugged? You've been mugged! Oh, you poor thing. Come on in, I'll call an ambulance."

"No, no please. I'm fine."

"Fine? You certainly are not fine! Have you seen yourself? Your poor face! No, you need an ambulance, and the police. I'll get the police. Come in… will you just come in?"

Pauline gingerly climbed the three old stone steps. Holding onto the door for support she made her way into the narrow hallway of the farmhouse.

Dolly took her arm and led her towards the open door in the cream painted wall. "Now, first of all, where are you hurt? Are you sure you don't want me to call an ambulance?"

"No, no, I'm sorry to disturb your evening, really I am. I just want to get into the house and have a bath actually…"

"Don't be ridiculous. You can't go off on your own. Let me at least get you a cup of tea and help you to clean up those wounds."

"Wounds." Pauline raised a hand and touched her swollen lips. The aches and soreness that she felt had become so much a part of every movement that she had given no thought to her appearance. "Is it bad? Does it look bad?"

"Well, I'm sorry, but yes. Whoever did this… Did someone do this? You haven't told me; what happened to you? Was it an accident or were you mugged?"

An escape was presented to her. In just those few words, several possibilities opened up and she searched for an answer that would be so much better than the truth. Then like a grey blanket exhaustion and defeat descended and she was just too tired and battered to begin to form the lies.

"No, I haven't been mugged. Oh Dolly, there's a man, dead. I killed him." As the words became reality her shattered spirit finally unwound into tears of fear and horror. Dolly flopped onto the settee beside her and wrapped her in a gentle hug as she sobbed. Great wracking gulps convulsed her trembling body. The other woman crooned soft, disbelieving murmurs.

"Now, now come on, come on. Don't be silly, calm down. Hush, hush."

As she regained control Pauline pushed back and took hold of both of Dolly's hands in hers. She drew in a deep, steadying breath. "I have Dolly! I couldn't help it. I think he was going to kill me, I really do, and I pushed him, oh God. He's in the rocks at the bottom of the cliff."

Uncertainty and disbelief met her gaze now. "What happened? Did he take you away? Oh no, no... have you been raped? Oh Pauline!"

"No, no. I haven't... he didn't. No. I don't know what to do next though."

"Well, we'll have to call the police. You do see that, don't you? If he took you away and there was an accident or... well... whatever happened, you have to tell them. They won't blame you, I'm sure they won't. Apart from that you know we have to get the coastguard, get him back. We can't risk someone finding him. Think how awful that would be? No, we must get some help." The sensible schoolteacher-like part of her took over now and Dolly stood and reached for a soft woollen blanket that covered a nearby chair. She wrapped it around Pauline's shivering shoulders.

"Now, I'm going to make you some hot tea. I'm going to send Jim up to the rocks so that he can get an idea about what has to be done; you know, to fetch the body back, and he can call the police." She turned and walked from the room shouting as she went. "Jim! Jim! Get down here will you? We need some help!"

Pauline laid her head back against the soft cushions and closed her eyes. Her mind raced. What was she to do now? To stick to the truth would expose the past lies or she could cover the mess with yet more subterfuge. For just one brief moment it seemed that maybe it would have been better had she been the poor broken body washing about in the waves at the foot of the promontory with all her troubles gone and finished.

Chapter 27

She wanted to be clean. The soft sleeping suit that she wore was stained and ripped. It was impossible to distinguish bruising from dirt on her hands and her nails were filthy and torn. She ran a hand through her hair and felt grit there in the salt laden strands.

"Dolly, please can you just give me a key and let me go and have a shower? I feel disgusting."

"I'm sorry my dear, the police were very firm on that. They'll be here soon, Jim has spoken to them and they are on the way. They said you weren't to try and clean yourself up before they've been. It's evidence you see."

"Evidence?"

"Yes, the way that you look, bits of stuff on your skin and your clothes. Oh, now don't cry, please don't. It's horrible I know, but it's for the best that they see you like this," she swept a hand towards where Pauline curled on the couch, legs drawn up under the blue blanket. "Well then they'll see, won't they, that you weren't to blame."

"I was though, I was. I'm to blame!"

"Now, come on, please don't do this to yourself. You've been through a terrible time. Don't wind yourself up. Of course you weren't to blame. I don't know what the world's coming to when innocent people can't even sleep in their beds without… well… this."

"Innocent? I'm not sure I am, Dolly! I didn't mean for any of this. I don't know how everything has turned out this way. I didn't think… I just tried to help and then I was afraid… but I did it, I pushed him and before that, earlier, I lied. If I hadn't lied in the first place this wouldn't have happened and they were such stupid lies, probably not even necessary, but I was scared."

"Now, come on. You're not making any sense and I think it's best if you just sit quietly and wait for the police. I'll make some more tea and how about a piece of toast? Could you eat a piece of toast?"

At the thought of food Pauline's stomach churned and she shook her head and gulped back the bile in her throat. "A cup of tea would be nice."

All she had tried to do was protect herself. Right from the start the lies had been only to hide from George. The accident and all the horror that had come from her one, kind action was still an unexplained nightmare. There had been no diamonds, no bag, no memory stick. She closed her eyes and concentrated on remembering the man when she had first found him, unconscious, his legs in the ditch. She remember the fear and panic. She had gone through his pockets looking for a phone but there had been nothing. She had only looked in his jeans anyway. Perhaps the things that he had lost were in his leather jacket? If that was the case, though, then where were they now? If the hospital had kept her jacket and handed it to him with its traitorous note inside then surely they would have returned his jacket to him as well?

So, someone else had removed the bag then. Surely not the rescue services, nurses, doctors; they were people to trust weren't they, not thieves and pickpockets. No, there must be another explanation. Perhaps the bag had fallen into the road and been swept away? It may be lying in the ditch even now. But would he not have gone there?

Surely he had looked? Now it was too late to ask him, even as the salt and grit dried in her hair the regret and self-doubt crept into her mind. She had handled this all wrong, hadn't she; everything she had touched had been tainted by her own desire for safety. Could she not have talked to him, logically and calmly? The horror was retreating now in the warmth of Dolly's home so Pauline began to second guess her actions and her shocked and confused mind filled with what ifs.

As thoughts chased puzzles through her head she rubbed her hands together and the chafing on her wrists spoke plainly of the truth. He hadn't wanted conversation and explanation; he was convinced that she had his property and his anger had been driven partly by fear. She had seen it in his eyes when he had screamed at her. The fog of confusion closed her lids and exhaustion lulled her to sleep before she realised that she had drifted away…

"Pauline, Pauline, come on my dear, wake up. The police are here. I've made some tea."

With a groan she came back to the world, pushed up from the slouch and turned to the doorway. A young woman in a dark suit and a tall uniformed police officer waited. "Have they found him? Have they got the body?"

The pair moved into the room and perched on the edges of homely old chairs. The woman leaned forward. "Pauline, may I call you Pauline? I'm Detective Ryan. I have to ask you some questions and see if we can sort out what's been going on here. Do you feel well enough? You look pretty beaten up; have you had a doctor look at you?"

"No, no I don't want that, I'm alright really. I just want to have a bath and get clean. Have they found him? Have they got him out of the water?"

"They're searching now."

"But, he's there, just in the water at the bottom of the cliffs. I can take you." As she spoke the words she prayed that they wouldn't ask her to follow through on the offer. She didn't believe she would be able to trudge back across the sands and make the climb and she didn't want to see him again rolling in the waves, bumping against the rocks.

"We have a team looking now, the lifeboat is there and the coastguard, but I have to tell you that up to now there is no body. We haven't found anything. Are you quite sure that was where he fell?"

Chapter 28

Pauline felt that she was teetering on the edge of insanity. There was now even more hell heaped on the torment she had already suffered. The side room at the hospital was bland and not quite clean. The medical team were calm and professional but without any warmth. Though the people searching had still not found a body, the possibility of murder or misadventure had meant that she must be "processed." It was an awful concept and a dreadful ordeal.

While she was examined, poked, prodded, scraped and questioned, her clothes were taken away and put in bags. At first they offered her a paper suit to wear in place of the hospital gown, but in the end Dolly was allowed to wait by the front door of the cottage until one of the forensic people brought her some of her clothes from the wardrobe and drawers at her cottage. It seemed that they didn't quite know how to treat her. She was so very obviously a victim and yet with no real evidence and only her confused account of events they didn't know whether she was a murderer or not. They were polite, kind and sympathetic to her wounds, but in the back of their eyes she could see suspicion.

However, it was clear to everyone that she was on the verge of total exhaustion. So, with the strong urging of the doctor and because she was now almost incapable of forming meaningful answers to any questions, they took her back to the farm. They had wanted her to stay in the hospital and she had begged to be allowed to leave. In the event they had no real means to make her stay. They had, of course, wanted her home address and because she didn't have the strength for anything else, she had given them the details of the house in The Dales. Trying to explain that she didn't live there anymore brought more tears so they gave up on the questioning and sent her away, "For now," they said, and the words chilled her.

She asked to go to the cottage but they were adamant. It wasn't possible; the little house was now a crime scene, tape covered the doors and it would be sealed while they combed the rooms for evidence of the intruder. What would they look for? There was nothing to find; just her clothes, a couple of books. She had so little; would that in itself cause them to be suspicious? She didn't know.

It was only the feel of Dolly's kind arms around her, and her gentle voice urging her to be calm, and promising a bed at the farm house that stopped her from falling apart completely. Then after it all; the hospital, the questions, the empty silences filled with puzzlement and disbelief, there was a drive home in the back of a police car with a silent driver and Dolly uncomfortable and embarrassed beside her.

At last she clambered between sweet smelling sheets in one of the neat little bed and breakfast rooms. A drug induced sleep carried her away, and while boats and police teams scoured the cliffs and beaches she slept, with Dolly creeping up the stairs at regular intervals to listen at the door and shake her head in confusion…

The house was quiet and calm. Pauline didn't want to open her eyes. If she could just stay where she was in the warm, dark place, maybe it would all go away.

Of course it didn't and in the end she knew it was time to drag herself back into the mess that had displaced her life.

She stretched her legs. The pain was similar to that after strenuous exercise; not too bad, bearable. She pushed herself up against the pillows and carefully swung round. She felt better than she had expected.

Her clothes were thrown on a chair and she vaguely remembered Dolly helping her to undress and pull on the T-shirt that she had on. Her mouth was dry and her tongue felt coated, the effect of the drugs she supposed. With the stiff movements and sighing groans of an old woman she rose to her feet and straightened her creaking back. A dresser stood against the wall; a mirror in a frame standing on the polished top.

She hadn't seen her face. Dolly told her it was bruised and battered but nothing could have prepared her for the wreckage that greeted her startled gaze. The skin around both eyes was blackened and swollen and her cheeks were multi-coloured with bruises. She had felt the swelling in her lips but hadn't been prepared for the sight of them; liver coloured with bruising and streaked with red where the skin had burst.

Though she knew it was all temporary – the doctor had assured her that most of it was superficial and would all heal – it was worse than any ruin George had caused. But of course he had been careful to hide his handiwork: he had expected her to live.

The tiny creak of the door had Dolly out of the kitchen and half way up the narrow staircase barely before Pauline had moved across the landing.

"How are you feeling? Take it carefully; here let me help you."

"Thanks. Actually, it's not too bad."

"You've been crying again, haven't you?"

"I saw my face. It's silly I know but…" She shrugged her shoulders.

"It'll mend my dear. You'll be surprised. It won't take long."

"Oh, I know. It's not that important really, not just now. Is there news, Dolly, have they found him?"

"I haven't heard anything. Nobody has been, but we are supposed to give them a call once you are up and about. There is just one constable now at the cottage; all the cars have gone. I don't know about the beach. Jim has gone out to see what's happening. He'll be back soon.

"Come on down and have some soup. You'll feel better with some food in your tummy."

"Oh, you are kind. I don't know what I'd have done without you. Thank you. And Dolly, I didn't mean to kill him. Well, I don't know what I meant; I just had to get away. You do believe me, don't you?" The moment of hesitation was brief but it was enough, no-one really knew what to think, not even this kind new friend.

It was time for truth. It was time to bring everything out into the light. "Can you call them for me, the police? I need to tell them everything that's happened. Before I do though, Dolly, I want to apologise to you. I haven't been completely honest, I am sorry but maybe when I explain you'll understand."

Pauline had made her way slowly down the steps and now Dolly reached a hand and gently squeezed her shoulder. "Whatever you've done, or said I'm sure you had your reasons. I think I'm a pretty good judge when it comes to people and I know you're not a bad person, Pauline. Come on, let's get on with it. You'll feel better when it's over."

When it's over. It would never be over. She would remember his screams forever. "Bitch! Bitch!" And the look in his eyes as he had scrabbled in the rocks for handholds and felt the cliff edge give beneath his panicked feet. No, some things were never over.

Chapter 29

She had expected it to be hard. Pauline told herself that after all she had been through the police with their questions would be difficult to face, but she would get through it. In the event it was far harder than she had imagined.

They still didn't know what to think of her. They had offered to bring a solicitor. The idea chilled her and she refused. Because she was still in pain from her injuries they had come to the farm instead of taking her to the police station. Their puzzlement had led them to be more gentle with her than she had expected but the kindness didn't lessen the guilt and the fear she felt.

It was calm and quiet in the lounge. A constable stood near the door. The hush was broken only with the sound of rain in the trees and splashing against the windows, and the occasional whoosh as a car passed on the wet road outside. Detective Ryan pursed her lips and shook her head, just a quick flick. She raised her eyes to meet the troubled gaze of the beaten, sad looking woman perched on the edge of the old settee.

"We haven't found a body. Teams have been out searching all yesterday and again this morning but there is no sign. So, either he wasn't dead and left under his own steam..." As Pauline opened her mouth to speak the policewoman raised a hand. "Or, there was no body, and that presents a puzzle of its own."

"He must have washed away. The tide took him."

"No, it's unlikely. We have had an expert from the coastguard consulting and – taking into account the time of year – when you say you last saw the body and the state of the tide it would be almost impossible for it to wash out to sea. You say it was caught in the rocks for one thing."

"Yes, yes it was. I called down to him, the water was turning him and moving him, but he was caught amongst the rocks. Yes."

"Exactly. And at this time of the year that is the high tide level so it would take a freak wave, or some other unlikely event to move him."

"Well, it could happen, couldn't it?"

"Yes, it could. But then the formation of the coast there means the body would wash to the other side of the bay and not out into open water.

"The thing is Pauline, if there is no body, there is no reason for you to have called us. But there are your injuries, which are obvious. Do you understand my dilemma? If what you are telling me is not true then it gives us a whole other set of problems. We have been trying to contact your husband on the number you gave us but haven't been able to get an answer. There is nobody at the address. Would you expect him to be there? Have you spoken to him yourself?"

So, there he was again: George. She was beginning to see, no matter how far she ran, no matter what horror she endured he would be there. She drew in a deep breath.

"I left him. I think I told you."

"Yes, I remember and we need to speak to him, to confirm that. We need you to clarify what exactly had happened because it is a rat's nest at the moment."

"I lied you see. I lied to the police."

"Ah. So, are you telling me now there was no body, no attack?"

"No, no you don't understand. I didn't lie to you. This isn't a lie. I lied before, to the police in Yorkshire."

"What police in Yorkshire?"

"I left home, well, left George, but he didn't know; he was away. That's why I chose to go just then. I had planned it all and I was coming here to hide. I've bought a house in France. That's where I'm going; the day after tomorrow it should be."

"Well, I have to tell you that at the moment it would be better if you don't plan on going anywhere out of the country. Not until this is all sorted out."

She hadn't understood. The uproar had been so loud in her life that she hadn't appreciated how her plans may be spoiled and her very future put in jeopardy. The realization was a physical blow. Drawing breath into her lungs, hanging on to a semblance of sanity, just holding on was all she could manage. Her hands were clasped in her lap, the knuckles white with tension and thoughts jittered and spun in her brain when she closed her eyes. Was there a way through this? If there was she couldn't find it, not right now, maybe not ever.

Her voice was swamped with tears as she forced out the next words. "Am I going to go to prison?"

Anne Ryan spoke quietly, slowly. "It's too early to say what is going to happen, Pauline. Right now all I have is confusion. Look, I need to ask you this and I know it might be tricky but you have to be honest with me. Have you ever had trouble with your nerves? Have you ever seen a psychiatrist, Pauline? Do you think this could be… well, do you think it might not have happened the way you think?"

They thought she was mad. As the spectre of mental illness was raised yet another path in the maze was opened.

Chapter 30

"Look, I think the only thing I can do here is to go back to the beginning. Well not quite... oh hell. Yes, the beginning." Pauline squared her shoulders. She drew in a breath and lowered her head. When she lifted her face again she looked across at Detective Ryan. Her gaze steady but her eyes flat, helpless.

"My husband beat me, he beat me often and I didn't tell anyone because I was ashamed and frightened. I stopped seeing my friends and I made a life that worked for me. In between the hell with George I had a life that I could live. I did my garden, I looked after the house and I spent hours and hours alone, walking in the hills. It was small and empty. All I had was the cat and my flowers." The tears had begun to flow as she had known they would but she swiped them away with a tissue and carried on.

"I put up with it for twenty years and then I had the chance to get away. I left, I didn't tell him I was going I just left."

Detective Ryan had tried to maintain an aura of cool detachment but the distress coming from the other woman in waves was making her uncomfortable. "Is it relevant to what has happened here, Pauline? Are you telling me that the dead man was your husband?"

"Will you just listen? Can you do that; just listen and I'll tell you? There was an accident on the road and I tried to help. I called the police, I held his hand, I sat in a sodding ditch and held his hand. I looked in his pocket for a phone, just for his phone."

"So, why did you lie, what was the lie?"

"I was afraid that if I gave my name and address that somehow it would get back to George and he would be able to find me. I was upset, I was scared, so I made up a phone number and I gave a false address. I'm sorry, okay? I'm sorry."

The police constable had stepped further into the room and the atmosphere was charged with emotion. Things were getting out of hand. Anne Ryan gathered her bag and folio together. "You're distressed, Pauline, this won't work. You need a solicitor, you need to calm down and come to the police station. I'll arrange it."

"No." Pauline shot from her seat and took the few paces to the door. She stood with her back to the old wood, her hands braced behind her. "No, listen to me. Let me tell you. You have to listen to me now."

The young officer and the detective shot a glance across the small space. Ryan held out a hand. "Alright, but try to keep calm. Come on back. Come and sit down, please just sit down." They waited until Pauline was perched, tense and watchful on the edge of the seat.

"I thought it would be alright. I listened to the news and they said that he was in hospital. After a while I put it behind me and I believed it to be over.

"Then the day before yesterday, in the night he came. I didn't know who he was at first. I had never seen his face because of the helmet. He was brutal, violent and he went on and on about diamonds, and a computer memory stick. It was like something out of a movie. I was scared, really scared, but I told him over and over that I had nothing, but he didn't believe me. He made me go with him, across the beach. There's a cave, over there in the rocks. He tied me up." She raised her arms to display the fading rope burns.

"He left me there all day while he went off somewhere. To see his clients, he said. When he came back I thought he would kill me and that is when I told him that I had buried the diamonds on the cliff walk."

"But, you said you didn't have them." For a moment Pauline simply stared at the constable. How could he be so dim? She shook her head.

"I had to tell him something! I truly thought my life was in danger and if I was outside I would stand more chance of either getting away or attracting attention." She took a deep breath and forged on. "I pretended to fall and when he came back I pushed him, I kicked him over the edge and he fell into the sea. I called to him and he didn't answer.

"I don't know where he is now; I don't know whether he is dead or alive but if he is alive then I can't stay here. You do see that, don't you? I can't stay here…" She dissolved into a flood of weeping. Her head was buried deep in her hands, a murmur escaped between quivering fingers, "I can't stay here. He'll come back and he'll kill me."

Chapter 31

"Don't get up, Pauline, you just sit there. I'll call through to Dolly, tell her we're leaving. I'm sorry but we will have to contact your husband. There's no way around it, but I don't see why we would have to tell him where you are if you don't want us to.

"I'll need to check with the police in Yorkshire about the rest of the story and then I'll come back. I have no idea where this is all going but with no body it leaves a conundrum. I need to get advice from other people. Try not to worry. On the other hand, we can't do much about the attack either and that's a worry. With all you told us about the bloke who abducted you, I'm not happy but am at a loss as to the next move for now."

"I don't care about it. I'm going to be fine. I just want this to be over. Do you think I can carry on and go to France?"

"No, I can't let you do that. Not until we get a better idea of what is happening. Put it off. Can you stay here?"

"I'll ask Dolly."

"If that doesn't work out could you go home, back to your house?"

"Have you not listened to anything I said? It took me twenty years to get out of there! Twenty years of being beaten and miserable, and you can actually stand there and suggest I go back!"

"Okay, okay, I'm sorry. Just see if you can stay with Dolly or in the cottage and if you can't, then let me know and we'll take it one step at a time."

As the two officers strode through the door, Pauline laid her head back against the cushions and closed her eyes. She was weary to the bone, her spirit was bruised and battered and although she knew she must struggle forward, all she could imagine was confusion and fear stretching forever. A wave of desperate sadness swept through her and it was only with a massive effort that she could push the grey blanket of depression aside.

Dolly stepped into the quiet room.

"Do you want some tea, Pauline? And a sandwich?"

"I'd love some, Dolly. And then, if you have a moment, can we have a chat? I have to try and work out what I'm going to do next."

"Ok. Now you rest here, I'll be back soon."

"Dolly, thank you."

Warm arms wrapped around her and the feel of Dolly's soft cheeks against her face was balm to her hurt and the kindness; although she had known Dolly for such a short time, it overwhelmed her and filled her heart with grateful tears…

"Well, the cottage is booked up from the end of the week and to be honest I don't think you should stay there alone anyway. Why don't you just bring your things over and stay in the house with Jim and me? I only let the rooms to bed and breakfast people so there's always a vacancy and it means I can look after you. I feel so guilty that all this has happened."

"Oh Dolly, none of this is your fault. Of course you don't really know the background do you?"

"Well only the bits I've overheard here and there. I know you left your husband but not much more than that."

"Okay, the least I can do is fill you in on what it's all about. Have you got a few minutes?"

"Of course."

Seated side by side on the sofa Dolly listened without comment as Pauline relayed the whole sorry tale.

"So that's all you know? This man who attacked you is the one from the ditch?"

"Yes, I don't even know his name. I know he was involved with some other people but I have no idea who they are."

"And you didn't see anyone else by the accident."

"No, it was quiet, the middle of the day and when I left home I just walked up the hill away from the village. Even the dog wasn't out at the farm."

Pauline let out a gasp and grabbed at Dolly's hand. "There was a car!"

"A car?"

"I've just remembered! I didn't ever think about it until now! As I left the house I had to get out of the way of a car, it was speeding through the village. I remember now thinking it must be a stranger because he was going far too fast for the road."

"Do you think it might be important?"

"Well, I don't know but they must have come down the same road as the motorbike and it was very soon after that when I found the accident. I wonder if perhaps I should tell the police anyway. I'll call them later, just in case."

"For now though, can I go over and bring some things back from the cottage and then tomorrow I'll move all my stuff here?"

"Oh, I don't think you should, it's not safe, or let me come with you at least. I'm waiting for a delivery for the shop but, maybe later."

"I think it's okay, Dolly, the place has been swarming with police and…" she shrugged, "I think he's dead, if it was the bloke from the cave you're worried about. I would like to go, it'll help me to settle – I really think it will."

"Well, I don't like it, not at all. It scares me. Call me if you're worried about anything, the house phone comes straight through to here and the shop. Oh, I wish you wouldn't go."

"Don't worry it'll be okay. I'll just bring my computer… oh no, not that; the police have it. Oh well, what I need for now and then tomorrow. I'll go and get the rest of my clothes and give you a hand to tidy up."

"Indeed you will not, in spite of everything you are still my guest and it's not your job to clean the place."

* * *

The air was fresh and as Pauline made her way across the wet grass she glanced towards the restless ocean and the rocks in the distance. She felt no fear as her eyes skimmed the dark shapes that were only rocks. It was the stranger who had caused her pain. She would not let man's evil impact on her delight at this lovely place. The many years as an abused wife had taught her that it was easier to overcome hardship if it was stowed in a box in your mind that could be pushed away, disallowed to spread and distort those things that were inherently beautiful: a summer sky, a sailing cloud or the sun sparkling on rippling waves.

There were marks on the cottage door where the police had brushed powder, looking for fingerprints and evidence of the intrusion. Pauline slipped the key into the lock and stepped into the dark hallway. Residual moisture dripped from the old gutters tinkling on cobbles and pathways outside and, looking through the old kitchen and beyond to the shimmering garden, she was tempted through and out into the small space.

She had expected to sense recent disturbance, but what she had not expected was the tingle up her spine and the ticklish feel of goose pimples on her arms and the absolute conviction that she was not alone. She spun around to look back towards the open door and caught a glimpse of a dark shadow on the dappled path.

Chapter 32

Was it a figure? A movement in the trees? Or just her overwrought mind? Her heart pounded.

The small gate to the beach was but a few steps away: if she ran now she may be able to reach the dunes and then try to make it back into the farm house. To do that she would need to turn her back on the house, the path and the dark shadows of the garden. She was petrified and for seconds couldn't drag her eyes away from the open door and the blind windows of the kitchen. Her mouth had dried and she gulped, desperate for moisture. Slowly, slowly she took one step backwards, then another. She dragged her feet along the old stones. her hands stretched behind her groping for the gate.

Another small step, then another. She could turn now and run but what if she tripped? Was the gate open? She couldn't remember. If she did get past the stone wall she knew the sand was soft and full of sharp grass: it would be hard to run.

She could scream.

If she screamed, Dolly might hear her, and Jim: they would come running, but would it be too late because whoever was in the house would hear her too and they were nearer.

Was there someone in the house?

Again she tried to peer into the dim rooms. The curtains in the little kitchen blew gently in a soft breeze, the door swung a little on the well-oiled hinges. Tree limbs creaked high overhead and a crow in the rookery shouted to the setting sun. The harsh noise caused her to start and a small sound, not quite a scream but more than a gasp, escaped her lips. She pressed her hand to her mouth.

It seemed that her heart would burst from her chest and her knees wobbled now, threatening to let her down just when it was essential that she was swift and sure.

She must move.

Was there anyone there?

The shout when she made it shocked her: she hadn't known she was going to speak until the words escaped her trembling lips. "Who is it? Who's there?"

The door moved again, slowly drawing inward and a figure appeared now, unmistakable. He was tall, dressed in jeans and a blue sweatshirt. His head was bald and his lower arms were covered with a pattern of tattoos. He stepped forward and held up his hands.

The rugged face was stern, blue eyes unblinking and he moved towards her. She turned from him. She would make for the gate and take her chances on the beach. Maybe there were walkers, someone to help her. She spun and as she did the intruder strode across the grass and reached his large hand towards her. He grabbed her upper arm, with strong, hard fingers. She saw the muscles in his arms flex as he held her, fighting against the pull of her body.

She twisted and brought up her hand to slap at his face, to try and scratch him. At the same time, she lifted her foot. Instead of pulling back now she moved forward, tried to judge the distance so that when she brought her knee up into his groin it would have all her strength behind it.

He saw the move. He knew what it meant and spun her around now with her back to him and his arm round her chest, above her breasts and he dragged her back to hold her tightly against his chest and belly.

"Don't scream, you don't need to scream. It's alright. I'm not going to hurt you."

Tears streamed from her eyes and as she opened her mouth to yell for help he clamped his fingers tightly across her jaw.

"Don't scream, you really don't need to be afraid. I won't hurt you. Keep calm."

She felt the heat from him through her T-shirt, the warmth of his arm across her upper body. She felt the tickle of breath in her ear as he leaned in close to speak again in his calm voice. "Don't be afraid, I won't hurt you. I'm going to move my hand now. Nod your head, tell me you understand and that you won't yell."

She nodded and slowly he released the grip on her face. "Okay, good, good. Now I want you to be very calm. I'm going to let you go. Please don't try and run, okay? Just nod."

She moved her head a small jerk and felt his arms loosen their hold. He kept her encircled but now she was barely contained. It would be possible to duck and run but knew that he would have her again before she made the gate. He spun her to face him.

He looked into her eyes. "Pauline, I need you to come into the house with me now. I need you to be calm and not to be afraid." She gave another sharp nod and he released his hold totally and stood aside gesturing toward the open door.

She moved past him and took the few steps back to the kitchen. He followed her inside and closed the door.

"Right, now please sit down, just sit at the table. We need to talk."

She shook her head. If she was seated she couldn't run and first chance there was she was going to run. "Please don't hurt me. I haven't got anything. I haven't got a bag of diamonds, or a computer memory stick. I don't have anything! Please don't hurt me."

The stranger moved to the other side of the table and to her surprise he dragged out the second chair and turned it to sit astride. He leaned his arms across the back and bent towards her. "I won't hurt you, Pauline. You are safe with me. Please sit down. I just want to talk to you."

Chapter 33

"Who are you? How do you know my name? What are you doing here?"

The hint of a smile danced across the stranger's mouth as his heavy brows rose with amusement. "Where would you like me to start?" He raised a calming hand as anger blazed now from Pauline's eyes in response to his flippancy.

"I'm Pete. Please." He gestured to the chair and as she lowered herself to the edge of the seat he let out a breath and leaned a little closer. His eyes were serious now as he looked directly into her face. "You've got yourself mixed up in something very dangerous. I know you didn't mean to. I know you don't have anything that you shouldn't; you didn't steal anything from Jed." Pauline tipped her head to one side, listening closely. He didn't frighten her so much, this large, rough looking individual, not the way the other man had done. He had a quiet about him that stilled the nerves and she felt the pounding of her heart slow. Outside the sun dipped into the ocean changing from sapphire to indigo as quiet waves rolled endlessly against the cooling sand, singing the song of evening.

"That's his name; the motorcyclist. I know you tried to help him and then what he did to you. I'm sorry for that. I made a mistake there. Stupidly I assumed he'd taken you with him so I followed him rather than looking on the headland. I know what happened to him also." She gasped and her hand flew to her mouth. So, was this to be blackmail? Retribution? Proof that she was a killer? Her stomach flipped as she tensed and moved to rise from the table.

Pete reached a hand across the small space and laid it on top of hers. "It's okay. He's dead, but you knew that didn't you? Please though, don't be afraid. You don't need to worry about it."

"Don't worry? How can I not worry? How do you know anyway? Who are you? Where is he? Have you got him… are you going to tell the police?"

"I am the police, Pauline. I'm not from around here, that's why I couldn't find you. If I'd been able to go to them they may have known about the cave. Although, having watched them searching for the body I'm not sure they do. That's where he was, for a while. I had to put him somewhere."

"Why, you should just have shown them, reported it."

"No. For the moment I don't want anyone to know he's dead."

"But, surely that's illegal. I mean isn't that illegal?"

"As I said, you've got yourself mixed up in something rather nasty. Okay, cards on the table. I am going to trust you. There's no other way. You're in danger: the whole thing is a mess and I think it's only fair that you understand. What I tell can only be between us. You won't be able to repeat this, do you understand?"

She nodded. Sat now with her hands in her lap, her eyes fixed on his, she waited. Whether she could trust him hadn't been decided but she would hear him out, give him a chance. What else was there to do?

"I'm undercover. You don't need to know all the details but the people Jed was working with are particularly nasty." He stopped and looked at the attractive woman sitting opposite to him, confusion and doubt creasing the skin between those rather lovely blue eyes. "Okay, let's see. I'm trying to decide how much you really need to know because the more you know the more danger there is."

She nodded, urging him on.

"I have been involved for over a year with a gang of people traffickers. Jed wasn't very important in the hierarchy. He was just a messenger and a bit of muscle when they needed it. However, he was carrying some very valuable stuff and he was playing a double game."

"The diamonds?"

"Yes, the diamonds. But also, and more importantly, the computer memory which has information on which, if it falls into the wrong hands – well I guess other wrong hands – will cause big problems for the people I am embedded with.

"I know you haven't got it, Pauline. I know who has. But that's another story altogether. The 'accident' that you were a witness to was no such thing. I don't suppose you noticed the amount of blood on the road?" Here she shook her head and pursed her lips. "No, I suppose it was all rather traumatic. But it was too much, way too much for a simple collision. Anyway, to cut a long story short, Jed didn't hit the sheep. The sheep was killed before he arrived and the blood and guts were spread across the road. There was also a wire; it was the wire that brought him off his bike. I know it'll haunt me that I couldn't help him but… in the bigger picture it makes a sort of sense."

"But… didn't the police in Yorkshire see that? Did they know about it?"

"No, God no. The thing is though, people are hitting sheep all the time on that road. It wasn't a puzzle, and though they went through the motions there was no reason for them to suspect anything. The wire was gone –

Jed wasn't supposed to survive but then you coming along just when you did screwed things up somewhat."

"There was a car. As I was leaving the village there was a car. Was that something to do with it?"

"Yes." I was in the car. I saw you. I knew it was going to create a problem. I tried to find you but you'd covered your tracks, hadn't you. You didn't make it easy for me."

"No. But I still don't understand."

"No, well, it's complicated. I don't know that it's worth going into too much detail. Look, Jed was… well… I suppose you could say he was ambushed by the people I am working with. They spread that poor dead sheep across the road. Then they left a bloke up there to wait and when Jed came off his bike he took the diamonds and the memory stick. He was supposed to finish Jed off but then but you came along and he had to leave him. It was a mess."

"I didn't see anyone else. There was nobody there but me and him, in the ditch."

Pete simply shook his head.

It didn't make any sense to her but Pauline was trying to understand. "But why don't you want people to know that he's dead?"

Pete gave a big sigh, he glanced around the kitchen. "Can I make us some coffee?"

"What? Oh, oh let me do it. I'll do it now. Look I think I'd better call Dolly, if not she'll come looking for me."

"I'll put the kettle on. You make the call." He smiled at her, a warm, sweet smile that shone out of the darkness of the last days like sun on the water. He was a good man; she instinctively knew that he would do her no harm so she relaxed and picked up the phone.

"Dolly, hi it's me. I just thought I'd let you know I'm okay. It's lovely over here and I just fancied a cup of coffee, I'll be back soon, okay?"

Pete was moving around the kitchen, searching in the cupboard for cups and coffee. He held up a packet of biscuits and wagged them in the air. Pauline smiled and nodded and was thrown by the idea that in less than an hour she had gone from trying to flee in terror to drinking coffee and eating Hobnobs with this man.

When they had their drinks, Pete shifted on the chair, preparing himself. He nodded to her, "Okay, let's see if I can make this make sense to you. The diamonds and so on belong to the nasties I'm in with. Jed worked for them. There is another crew and guess what, he worked for them as well." Here he gave a short and bitter laugh, "Honour among thieves; what a laugh! When money's involved, there's precious little honour anywhere with these clowns. Anyway, my group, I have to call them that but believe me I'm kosher, I'm not bent. Let's call them group A, A for Assholes – yes, that works..." He looked at her waiting for a sign that she believed him. She smiled in the gathering dusk, waved a hand for him to continue.

"Right, so Jed was on his way to group B; let's call them that. So my lot, the A's wanted their stuff back and they wanted rid of him."

"So, the accident?"

"Yes indeed. It would have worked except Jed didn't die and he believed that you had his stuff. He was told, erm, by group B, that you have them, Pauline." He leaned to her and laid his warm hand over hers where she gripped the cup. "Those people are going to come after you once they know he is dead. They believe that you have the diamonds and more importantly the memory stick. If we can keep his death a secret for a while it will buy us some time; they will assume he is still trying to get the items from you. Once they find out he's dead then they'll come after you. I don't want that, Pauline. I am going to have to wind this thing up. We can't put you at risk."

"Oh, I'm sorry." It was ludicrous; here she was in the middle of something that she would never in her wildest dreams have thought possible and she was apologising for first of all helping to save some vicious criminal and then for having killed him. From somewhere deep inside the insanity of it all spilled over and – perhaps in reaction to the emotion of the last hour – she began to giggle. Before long her eyes were streaming as she hiccupped and gasped for breath and a bald, tattooed giant stood across the table gazing at her in disbelief and wonder.

Chapter 34

The laughter, though rather hysterical, had done Pauline a world of good. She shook her head.

"I'm sorry, I really am. I know there is nothing funny going on here it's just – Oh I don't know… the whole thing is so – insane and unreal. This sort of thing – all this sort of thing just doesn't happen to people like me. I'm ordinary. Just quiet and well – ordinary." She shrugged her shoulders.

"I do see what you're saying, Pauline, but believe me; this is very real. I can't stress enough that you mustn't tell anyone what I have just shared with you. Not the lady at the farm."

"Dolly."

"Yes, Dolly, and not that odd bloke that lives with her."

"Jim. Yes he's a bit odd, but I think he's okay and he's been very nice to me while I've been there."

"No matter how nice they are you mustn't tell them anything. It would put them in danger. Do you understand me?"

"But… they haven't done anything. They don't know anything about all this."

"But they know you and it's enough to mark them." Pete stepped around the table and crouched in front of her. "Look, I know this will scare you and I'm sorry for that, but you have to believe me when I tell you that these people are very dangerous. They are ruthless: they don't care who gets hurt. They make their living trading in people. Human beings are no more than a commodity to them. They won't hesitate to take any and all measures to protect themselves.

"I am trying to arrange to have you taken to a place of safety, but until then…"

Pauline's sharp intake of breath caused him to pause mid-sentence.

"You're what! You are doing what!? Taken to a place of safety!? Who the hell do you think you are? I'm not an infant! I'm not a, what did you say, a commodity! How dare you?" She spun away from the chair and paced to the door where she snatched up her bag. "You are trying to arrange… Well don't you bother. I will go where I decide. I spent the last twenty years of my life being told where I could and couldn't go and I've finished with that. I can't believe it. You can just stop trying to have me 'taken' anywhere. Bloody hell!"

"Hey, hey. Calm down. Have you been listening to anything I've said here? Your life is in danger, that's the truth of it. You could end up dead. Once these people find out that Jed is dead they are coming after you. Before that happens I have to make sure that you're safe. Have you the slightest inkling what can happen? Do you want to end up in pieces, sliced and diced and thrown onto a landfill in a black plastic bag? You thought what Jed did to you was bad. Well let me tell you he was taking great care of you. He thought you were of value to him, Jed was a pussy cat compared to some of the people I'm mixing with right now. You have no say in this thing Pauline. You have to be kept safe."

She could find no words to throw back at him. She was aghast and furious and yet speechless.

"You can go back to the farm tonight. I'm going to be just outside."

"What do you mean just outside?"

"I'm going to be keeping watch tonight, I daren't risk them coming looking for Jed and maybe finding you."

"How could that happen? They don't know who I am, where I am."

"Oh, believe me they can find out. I found you; not soon enough to save you from the cave but I found you."

"Yes, but you're with the police."

"There are more ways to find someone if you want to than just the police. Jed found you."

"Well yes, but he had my jacket."

"Oh, come on, I found you and he did. We don't know what he's told his mates. You're vulnerable and we have to protect you."

"Well, where am I going to go?"

"I don't know yet, I have some colleagues working on it but it's a bit complicated with me still in the field. Look, for tonight go back to the farm. I'll be outside and as soon as possible we'll get you away."

"But what about France? What about my house there?"

"I'm sorry, Pauline, but for now that's just going to have to be on hold."

"But they don't know about that."

"They may know and anything they don't know they can and will find out. Will you listen to me please?" He had come close now and reached a hand forward to lay it on her upper arm. "I'm sorry. I know this seems very unfair but it'll be over soon. I'll keep you safe."

A warm tide swept her body and her heart hitched just once. How many times she had longed for someone to say just those words to her! Standing here in this little cottage with her world turned on its head they had fallen from the lips of the most unlikely character she had ever met. They melted the residual anger and soothed down her nerves and she found herself smiling up into his eyes.

"Ok, I'm sorry. I didn't mean to be difficult. It's just all rather upsetting."

"I know. Come on, let's get you back to Dolly and Odd Jim. Stay in the house and try not to show yourself too much. When I need to speak to you again I'll let you know."

"How?"

"Oh, don't worry about that. I have my ways." And with a wicked little grin he turned and opened the door. Holding up a hand to indicate that she should wait he stepped outside. He glanced back and forth across the road and garden and listened to the silence for a while before waving her forward.

They walked together the few yards to the farm. "Try not to worry, Pauline. This will soon be over, I promise you." He threw an arm around her shoulder in a sort of friendly half hug and then pushed open the wooden gate to let her through. As she made her way across the cobbles she could feel his eyes watching her and his presence 'keeping her safe.' It warmed her and she was surprised by the thrill of something approaching excitement deep in her gut. She grinned to herself. For some unaccountable reason, in the midst of all this turmoil, she felt happy.

Chapter 35

"Oh, my word, I was getting so worried! Are you alright? You look a bit flushed."

"I'm fine, I'm fine, Dolly. It was just lovely over at the cottage. Peaceful you know, and I took a little time. I hope you weren't worried."

"Well, I don't know. The last few days have had me so upset. I wonder if you have a few minutes spare? Can we have a little glass of wine and a chat?"

"Well, yes of course. Dolly, I have to tell you that I can't thank you enough for what you've done for me. I would never have brought all this trouble to your door but you've been such a friend. I'll never forget how lovely you've been."

"Oh, now come on don't be getting upset. Don't cry. Come on let's have a drink."

"Can we sit in the garden, that little private bit at the back, behind the barn? It's such a lovely evening. You know I used to come to Cornwall so much when I was little and over the years I had forgotten how magical it can be. All this drama could have spoiled it but meeting you and receiving such kindness, it's made me determined to somehow handle all this, you know, not let it spoil my memories."

"Well, I only did what anyone would do and yes, I know what you mean about the magic. I missed the place such a lot when I was away and when I lost my husband, Bill, I just wanted to come home.

"Will you ever go back to your husband do you think?"

"No, no definitely not. He used to hit me."

"Oh, my word. You poor thing. It's despicable, absolutely unforgiveable. Was it him? Was it your husband who sent that awful man, the one who took you away?"

"Oh… no… no it wasn't him; not George. That was all to do with something else."

"But, why – I mean why did that happen? Oh no, no you don't have to tell me. I shouldn't be asking. It's just so – well so odd and unexpected. That sort of thing doesn't happen here; thugs and kidnappers. Of course we have our bits of robberies and so on but nothing like that. When I think about it, you over there in that awful cave all day and then struggling back on your own all bruised… oh, it makes my blood boil."

"Hey, come on it's all over. Let's take these glasses outside and enjoy the peace."

Sitting on the little flagged patio in the early dark, listening to the quiet shush of waves on the beach and the cry of an owl hunting in the woods soothed and quietened Pauline. It should have been bliss; it would have been if the shadows hadn't held such threats and the rattle of dried grass on the dunes hadn't sounded so very like footsteps and if only a tall, bulky man with a bald head and kind eyes had been standing close and keeping her safe.

"What are you going to do Pauline?"

"Do?"

"Yes, you can stay here as long as you like. I hope you know that. You can stay here until you are ready to go on to your new place in France – or whatever you are planning now. The thing is though; you must be so confused with everything that's happened."

"Oh Dolly. I hope you know that I'm going to pay for my room and everything, is that… erm… is that what you were thinking? I suppose it's best we clear that up right now. I want you to charge me whatever you would take for that room. Good heavens, I owe you so much more than that and I wouldn't dream of you being out of pocket. Now we must be clear, yes?"

"Well, that wasn't what I really meant but yes, I suppose we should clear that up. Now, you can't pay me what I would usually charge, I wouldn't hear of it. But we'll perhaps come to some agreement. I would let you stay in the cottage, if you wanted, but it's been booked for a long time and… well…" Here a shrug of the shoulders was enough to convey the problems and commitments of the service industry and Pauline leaned over and gave Dolly's hand a gentle squeeze.

"It's fine, Dolly, really. I love being in the farmhouse and if I can just stay for a few more days and then…" as the words left her lips she realised that she had no 'and then.' There was just now, this hour today and no knowing what tomorrow would bring.

"Are you cold, Pauline? Are you shivering?"

"No, I'm not cold it's just… oh what do they say; someone walked over my grave."

"Oh… I don't like that expression. It always seems so very sinister."

"Yes, I suppose it is. Hey, let's not get down. Cheers, Dolly. Here's to the future."

"Yes, yes that's better. To the future, whatever it may hold."

Their glasses chinked and the wine glowed in the moonlight. Pauline wondered if perhaps that were an even more sinister thought than the old wives' tale about graves and shivering. Her stomach flipped as she thought of the secrets and the threats and the strangeness that had overtaken her and which seemed now to be no nearer an end.

Chapter 36

There was no air. Her lungs screamed for it. Water tickled at her legs and she felt it rise, above her ankles, her knees, sliding upwards silken against her flinching skin. Sightless eyes strained against the dark. She was blind, blind and gasping and desperate. High above a tiny light beckoned. She reached but her hands were caught. She tried to turn. Her body was held. A scream gathered in her throat, locked there by the terror.

She had thought that it was over. Surely she had escaped the cave and the horror? She thought that he was killed. "Bitch! Bitch!" There was the shutter of small rocks, the fear and the blame. "Bitch! Bitch!" As her body tossed and twisted the bonds grew tighter and the darkness gathered close.

The pain of burning lungs jolted her into wakefulness.

The lurch from nightmare to the dimness of her little room brought with it only more terror. The hand across her mouth, fingers hard against her cheeks was a greater menace than the lack of air in her dreamscape; for this was real. She no longer wanted to reach for the tiny glow as the torch beam probed the gloom. Every instinct urged her to turn from the light, but the grip on her face and the weight across her shoulders disabled her more than the ethereal bounds of the dissipating dream had done.

"Pauline, shush. Pauline, don't scream. I'm sorry, It's me. It's Pete."

He shone the torch to his face. Angled it so that she could see him; a deep shadow towering over her with the moon of his face terrifyingly lit from beneath. Deeps and planes and shadows, a mask of horror.

"Okay?" She nodded and even as he released his grip she pushed up and away. "I'm sorry, I didn't want to frighten you but we have to go. We have to go now."

"Go? I'm not going anywhere. How did you get in here? Where's Dolly? Where's Jim?"

"They're okay. They're asleep. Come on, we haven't time for this. Get some clothes on."

"No, no... I'm not going anywhere with you. How do I know who you are? I only know what you told me. I'm staying here. Get out, leave me alone! I don't want to be a part of this, any of this."

"I know," he sighed and stepped back from the bed as she swung her feet to the floor, unwilling to be disadvantaged by her position. "I know, but please, I need you to come with me."

"No." She opened her mouth, drew in a deep gasp of air. As he perceived her intent to yell he flicked a hand behind his back. The gleam of dull metal and the unmistakeable shape of the weapon petrified her. Sweat trickled down her back and her stomach lurched.

"I'm sorry, Pauline. Shit. Look, I'm not going to hurt you. I'm trying to make you safe. You really need to trust me. You can trust me." As he spoke he stretched his hand towards her and flipped the gun around, offering her the handle. "Here, take this." Shuffling backwards across the narrow bed she shook her head and held up her hands warding off possession of the killing thing.

"No, don't do that. I don't want to touch that."

"Then please, just get dressed. If I was going to hurt you I could have done it by now; don't you see?"

Ever watchful she clambered to the floor and scuttled, bent at the waist, her hands protectively crossed on her chest. She dragged open the wardrobe door. She glanced back and he had turned away.

Her heart began to settle. She took in a calming breath. He had turned away to allow her privacy, dignity.

The wooden hangers rattled across the rail causing him to hiss in frustration and so with greater care she grabbed some clothes, jeans and a warm sweatshirt, and dragged them over her shivering limbs.

"Where's your bag? Your phone?"

"All stolen. They were on the beach."

"Shit. What was in it? What was on the phone? Oh, don't worry. Tell me later." He reached and took hold of her hand.

"There was nothing. It was all blank. I was hiding."

"Of course. Well that's a blessing. Come on."

"Where… where are you taking me?"

"We have to just get out. My cover is blown and they know where you are."

"How? I haven't told anyone anything. I didn't tell Dolly."

"I know, I know. It's somewhere else. A leak. I don't know yet but we have to go."

"What about Dolly and Jim?"

"I'll contact the local force when we've gone. They'll take care of them."

Down the darkened staircase and out into the fragrant dawn. He gripped her hand, guided her to a car hidden in the field gate and held the door as she slid inside. As they turned to the road the sun tipped the horizon with faint pink light and a new day began.

Chapter 37

"Pete, where are we going? What are we doing?"

"I'm making you safe. There'll be a place."

"What sort of place? I haven't got any stuff with me. How long will we be there? What am I going to do afterwards? Pete, I'm scared."

He didn't turn. The roads were tortuous and wet, illuminated in places by the rising sun. Moisture evaporated in the warming air and a small mist formed. Clouds of vapour floated several feet from the ground. The way was bordered by deep hedges and walls. In full daylight, at leisure, it would have been difficult driving; now it was perilous. They were travelling so quickly and though he seemed a good driver, confident and calm, Pauline gripped the door handle, her fingers tight around the plastic.

"I know, Pauline, I am so sorry about all this. You must be confused and I understand that you are scared, but just bear with it. I do have a plan." He gave a short snort of a laugh and shook his head. "Well… sort of."

"Oh, great! Well, that gives me a lot of confidence I must say!"

"No, no really I do. It's fine. Look, you can help. Open the glove box." She leaned forward and clicked open the lid. Dim light gleamed in the grey space.

"It's empty… oh no, wait, there's an instruction book for the radio. Oh well that's good, we'll be able to have music." The flippant comment caused Pete to glance at her and his teeth flashed in a grin.

"I like you, Pauline. I do." A ridiculous glow of warmth spread from her belly and she was glad of the darkness for she was sure she was blushing. The unaccustomed emotion unnerved her, caused her to snap at him.

"Oh, that's good to know. That makes a huge difference." Again the little snort of laughter.

"Can you look right at the back, down in the left hand corner there should be a bit of fabric. It just looks like a bit of the lining sticking up. Can you see it?"

The seat belt cut into her shoulder as she leaned towards the dashboard. Her fingers feathered along the back of the compartment and found the tag. It was little more than a thread. "I've found it I think… but what is it? it's just like a bit of cotton."

"Yeah, that's it. You should be able to pull it and the back will come loose. You have to do it slowly or it twists and that's a bugger."

"Well, if you keep throwing the car around the bends I can't even keep hold of the thing. Can you slow down a bit do you think?"

"Okay, okay. Have you got it now?"

"Yes, yes it's coming." The plastic panel slid out and she held it on her knee and peered back into the expanded space. The dull gleam of metal unnerved her. If he was going to ask her to touch the gun he was on a hiding to nothing. She hated them and nothing would entice her to take it from its moulded rubber housing. "I'm not passing you that. Is it loaded? God that's two guns you've got! What the hell is this all about? I thought you were with the police?" As she spoke the words a cold chill ran down her spine and took her breath. He registered the gasp.

"Don't panic. Really Pauline, please don't panic. I've told you I'm not operating in the open. I promise you that you are in no danger from me. Truly.

"Look to the right there should be a phone in a little box. Can you see it?"

"Yes, oh yes, I have that."

"Great. Take it out and turn it on would you."

The little machine beeped cheerfully as tiny pinpricks of LED lights sparkled under her hand.

"He glanced away from the road for a moment and the thud of tyres and judder of the car coaxed a squeal from her throat. "Shit, shit, sorry. Hedgehog."

"Oh no." Tears sprang to her eyes as she turned to peer backwards to where the tiny body lay on the tarmac, its life ended by a moment's inattention.

"I'm sorry, Pauline. It would have been quick."

She couldn't speak but simply nodded dumbly and bowed her head to concentrate on the phone, opening the contacts screen.

"There's only one number on here, Pete."

"Yup. Can you pop it into the hands free cradle and connect for me? Shit, another of the spiny little sods, what's the matter with them. It's okay, I missed it."

As she grabbed for the dashboard to steady herself Pauline found herself smiling. "Well done."

"Yeah right. Can we make the call now do you think?"

"Sorry, okay. She poked at the button and the call tone buzzed faintly. After two rings a voice filled the car. "Pete?"

"Yeah. With one other soul. I need a bolt hole."

"Hold."

For long minutes there was nothing, though she could feel the tension in his body and sensed impatience from the increased rate of his breathing. Was he afraid? If he was then what could the future hold for her? For both of them? As one thought followed the next a worm of fear writhed in her gut. How had she managed to find herself in this bizarre situation and then, would she have been better staying with George? Should she have settled for that life as miserable as it had been, rather than this? At least back then the danger and violence were familiar; not this unlooked for dread, this rising fear and unforeseen threat.

She glanced at the solid form of the man beside her, the man who had promised to keep her safe and she leaned back against the seat. Let it be, she thought. Just let it be.

Chapter 38

A disembodied voice filled the car. The reception was rattly and faint, the banks and hedges perhaps obstructing the signal. After a brief conversation, most of which was unintelligible to Pauline, Pete rolled his shoulders and his grip on the wheel seemed less tense.

"Is it okay now?" She couldn't even imagine what "it" or "okay" might be but felt desperate for reassurance.

"Yeah. I know where we're going. It's about two hours. Can you take the phone out of the thing?"

"Do you want it back in the glove box?"

"No, you need to open it up. Can you do that?"

"Well of course I can. I'm not stupid."

"No, I know, that wasn't what I meant. Oh whatever, just open it will you." So, there it was. The short fuse. It was a clear indication that, no matter what he said, things were far from okay.

"Okay, now what?"

"Take out the SIM, fling it through the window. Then the battery, then the phone. If you can break it up a bit first that would be even better."

Cold air took her breath and her hair swirled in the draught. She flung the plastic bits as far as she could. "Okay. That's gone."

"Well you might as well settle back if you can. There's nothing more we can do now except cross our fingers." All that was left was to hand over her fate and her future to Pete. So, she pushed back in the seat and turned her head to watch as the wakening world flew past to be lost behind them as he drove on to whatever their fate would be.

After another half an hour they hit the motorway. Now they were simply one more in an never-ending trail of cars and lorries thundering through the landscape. The ride became more even. In spite of everything, Pauline felt her head begin to nod and as clouds filled her brain she reclined the seat a little and let herself drift off.

"Pauline, come on. We're here."

She'd had no idea what to expect. All there was to imagine was from films and television; she had thought maybe a grimy flat, a fortress somewhere in the country, or even perhaps a police station.

Peering through the car window she was surprised to see a neat semi. A young mum pushed a buggy along the pavement and a ubiquitous parcel delivery van was parked just a little further along the road. It was ordinary, normal and in fact rather boring.

"Where are we?"

"Uh… I guess you could just say 'somewhere'. It's not that important and actually it's better if you don't know too much. Just in case."

"In case?"

"Well, you know, it's a sort of secret and well…" She fixed her gaze on him but he couldn't look at her and glanced away awkwardly.

"You mean in case I'm forced to tell someone don't you? You think I'm going to be caught or something and they'll… what? Torture me? Bloody hell. Just what have I got myself into here? I wish I'd left that bloke where he was, in the ditch."

"Yeah, to be honest, so do I."

It wasn't his fault though, was it. It wasn't his fault and he was doing his best. "Oh, come on, let's get on with it." She swung open the car door and uncurled onto the pavement. Her muscles still suffered from the damage inflicted in the cave and on the rocks so she stretched her arms above her head, easing the stiffness.

Pete came round and took hold of her arm, "Hey come on, let's get inside."

"What am I going to do about clothes? How long am I going to be here? Pete?"

"Hmm." He was crouching now, retrieving a key from under a flower pot.

"I can't believe that. You're not supposed to do that. Don't you know that's the first place they look, criminals and so on."

He grinned at her. His smile creased the weathered skin around his eyes and lifted the muscles of his face. Blue eyes sparkled. "I know. Quite right. Though in fairness these will only just have been put here."

"Right."

"Did you want to ask me something?" He had pulled her into the narrow hallway and now turned back to the door. There was a bank of bolts and locks which he spent time securing and she noted that the glass, though pretty and ornamental from the outside was reinforced on the inside by a metal grill.

Now that they were indoors, Pauline was overcome by a sense of intimacy, a wave of shyness. She dipped her head, clasped her hands in front of her. She unfolded them and let them hang at her sides. Her arms didn't know what to do; she folded them across her front. "I, erm... I just wanted to ask... Will you be staying with me? Well, what I mean is... you're not going to leave me are you? I don't want to be on my own." She raised a hand; the need for human contact, for a reassuring hug was overwhelming.

He tipped his head to one side, moved a half step closer. His hand brushed her arm and then her fingers were folded in his great, bear like paw. "Don't worry, Pauline. I'll be here. I'm staying."

The gentle tug was all that she needed to take her into the fold of his embrace and as the heat from his body soothed her aching muscles his presence soothed her aching soul. Her heart juddered, part delight and part sadness, for this wasn't real. This closeness was fleeting, but it showed her what had never been hers and she grieved for the loss of what she hadn't had and now never would have: a man, kind and careful of her, just another person to be with.

Chapter 39

They moved through the quiet rooms. Pete's hand stretched behind him, silently holding her back. He had taken out the small gun and as he scanned the empty spaces, Pauline had to bite back the urge to giggle. It was fear and nerves of course, but all so unreal it felt silly. Some strange play-acting reality divorced from the real world of Pauline Green. It was so much outside her world of gardens and shopping, of endless lonely walks and bitter mornings after nights of violence. This was a joke, surely just some outrageous comedy that had inadvertently drawn her in.

In time he had walked into every room downstairs. "Okay, seems fine down here. I'm going up so you stand in the hall and be ready to move."

She cracked; it was all too much. She raised her voice to cry out, "Hello, anybody up there? Pete's got a gun and he's coming to get you!"

He hissed at her and spun on the step. "What the hell…"

"Oh, come on. If there'd been anyone there they'd have come and shot us by now!" She pushed past him and stomped up the blue carpet. "Come out, come out!"

All he could do now was laugh. In truth he had to acknowledge that some of the performance had been for her benefit. The thought shamed him a little and he felt heat rise to his face. He ran up the stairs after her. It felt good to laugh but he had to make sure that she understood the danger.

"Okay, okay, very funny. But really, you have to listen to me. We have to be careful until this is sorted."

For her part Pauline had surprised herself. Really it was so unlike her but she had taken all that she could of continual tension. If there had been gunmen, gangsters or whatever hiding in the bedrooms she would have been responsible for heaven knows what carnage but the whole ludicrous situation had pushed her to the edge and she had leapt over. It felt good. She felt free and actually a bit brave and carefree.

Since her marriage she had lost the girl she used to be, the one who rode her bike at breakneck speed down the hills near home. She had swum in open lakes, canoed in white-water rapids, enjoyed rock climbing and had camped on her own in the hills. She hadn't been afraid. The fear had begun the first time George had raised his hand to her and increased with each blow and every new betrayal.

A fizz of confidence bubbled through her and she found herself grinning as she turned to watch the solid figure join her on the landing.

"Okay, bedrooms. Pick one. There should be some basics in the bathroom and some food in the kitchen. How about if we make a bite and then we can talk about what comes next. How would that be?"

"Yeah. I don't mind which room." As she spoke Pauline pushed open the doors, there were three rooms equipped with beds, wardrobes and dressers. All were fairly basic but clean and the beds were all made up ready to be used. "I'll take this one, it has twin beds. I think you might be more comfortable in the double, you're bigger than I am."

"That's kind. Thanks. I have to say it'll be nice to have a decent bed to sleep in for once."

"Right. This one has an en suite bathroom. Oh yes, and there are toothbrushes, soap and stuff. Crikey, there's even a dressing gown! Is this what my tax money pays for?"

"Uh, I guess so. I'd never thought about it... but yeah, I suppose."

"I'd love to have a shower. Do you think the water's hot?"

In answer he pushed past her to turn on the washbasin tap. After a few seconds steam began to rise from the white porcelain.

"Brilliant. I'll have a shower and then see what I can cook us to eat. Is that okay?"

"Yeah, great. In the meantime I'll pop out into the back garden. There's a shed out there and though I know you think it's all a great laugh I do need to check it out."

"I'm sorry, it's just that it all seemed to be so very dramatic. It's not the world I live in, not really."

"Well, maybe I was going just a bit over the top. I was trying to impress you. The least you could have done was fainted."

With a grin he turned and she heard his feet thunder down the stairs and then the rattle of locks being drawn back.

The rush of water from the shower head drowned out any other sound as she stepped under the hot torrent and felt the tension melt from her muscles.

Chapter 40

There were sachets of shampoo and conditioner, tiny single use bottles of body balm and a small tube of toothpaste.

As she rubbed herself with the surprisingly fluffy towels, Pauline mused anew at the strange events that had brought her to this moment. The bath robe was cheap and thin but it was clean and still in the manufacturer's bag. She tore away the polythene and then, wrapped in the warm softness, she made her way back into the bedroom.

Using the hair dryer provided, with the aid of a brush from her handbag she was able to give her short hair some body, although she wished she had thought to bring her own toiletries as they left the farmhouse.

Was it less than a day ago since the tense drive; the poor dead hedgehog?

In the drawer she was amazed to find some cheap knickers, still in the packet and a T-shirt which she could use for sleeping.

In spite of it all, the shower, the time to herself and the normality of standing in the simple tiled space had done much to raise her spirits. As she made for the stairs, a smile lifted her lips and brightened her eyes.

This felt incongruously like a stolen holiday. It was a small adventure. Though the way here had been nasty and frightening, with Pete to look after her and his promise that it would be over soon, she felt optimistic. She would be ready to cross the Channel on schedule or at the very most a few days late.

She liked him and would put herself in his hands. He was so different from all the other men she had ever met: rough and slightly scary but with kindness deep in his eyes. She sensed a gentleness about him at odds with the tough exterior. She hadn't been alone with many men apart from George; he hadn't allowed it and she felt like a giddy girl now; alone with a strange and dangerous male. It was exciting.

She was looking forward to making him a meal. It would be fun to root around in the kitchen cupboards and the fridge to find what they might have been provided with. She supposed eggs; there were always eggs. The holiday cottage welcome pack had eggs, cheese and milk. How long ago that seemed now with all the horror that had come since the first magic night by the coast.

"Pete?" She made her way through to the kitchen and then back down the hallway into the lounge. "Pete?"

He must be still outside checking the shed.

She pulled open kitchen cupboards. They were simply equipped, again like a holiday place. It was all so temporary and here and there scuffs on the walls and scratches on the paintwork witnessed the passing of other tenants.

There were indeed eggs in the fridge and bacon, a pack of ham and some salad. If he liked omelettes then maybe... She gave a tiny snort of laughter. Again her life was reduced to a film or a television drama; the ubiquitous omelette. There was no wine, she was disappointed. To complete the set there should be cheap wine or at least a quarter bottle of whisky.

"Pete?" She had pushed open the back door. How long did it take to check on a shed?

It was at the end of the garden, beneath a brick wall. A small flagged path dissected the neat lawn. There were no flower borders but a couple of shrubs broke up the monotony of the little space. "Pete?"

The little quiver of fear was so small at first that she called it hunger. "Pete, are you there?"

Perhaps she shouldn't be out here calling in the open. She didn't want him to be angry with her and this probably wasn't sensible. She stepped back inside and pulled the door closed. Crossing to the window she peered out into the garden. There was no sign of him.

In the lounge she stood behind the heavy drapes to squint out through old-fashioned net curtains to where the car sat at the curb. He wasn't there. Her throat had dried and the quiver of nerves shuddered through her gut.

As her feet thudded on the carpeted stairs, she remembered his grin as she had pushed past him such a short while ago, "Come out, come out," she had said. Had they? Had they come out while she was in the shower?

On the landing she paused to listen; perhaps he was in the master bathroom. There was no sound of running water but then the click of a handle turning echoed through the house.

She ran into her chosen room at the back and stared out. Now at the end of the grassed and paved garden she could see the shed clearly. She could see the door as it swung on shining metal hinges. She could see Pete, and she could see the man beside him and the glint of dark metal in his hand and she heard the fall of feet on the stairs.

Chapter 41

She glanced around. The wardrobe door stood open. Should she climb inside? It was empty and the very thought was ridiculous. The curtains were short, offering no chance of concealment. The room was so simple and sparse that there was nowhere to hide.

The stairs creaked and she scurried back to glance through the window. Pete was at the end of the little path. He and the man with him were staring at the house. Pete shook his head, he lifted his hands and gestured. There was tension in every line of his body.

She had to hide.

She had to help him.

Now there was movement on the landing. A small tin of deodorant stood on the dresser. She grabbed it and snapped off the plastic cap.

She chose the bed, the hiding place of frightened children. As she slithered underneath, the door to the room next door slammed back against the wall.

Even with the covers dragged as far down as they would come it was hopeless. Like a creature in the jungle she had fallen into a trap. No way out. Nowhere to go. She lowered her head to her hands, closed her eyes. Her stomach clenched in fear.

The booted feet and lower legs were visible now in the glow from the window on the half landing. Pauline tried to remember what she had left in the room. Was it obvious that she had been there? Well, of course it was. There was a damp towel, a steamy bathroom filled with the scent of shampoo and body spray. There might as well have been a great arrow pointing to her hiding place. It was all over. This was the end and Pete wasn't here. She really would have liked to be with him now. To face this horror alone seemed an unduly harsh twist of fate but then had she not been alone for twenty years?

The intruder didn't call out. Feet paused briefly before the wardrobe and the door swung open. Next was the bathroom and the overwhelming evidence of her occupation and then it was time. The black boots were inches away from her face. They flexed and bent. She held the small can in front of her.

There was a small change in his breathing as he leaned down. The bedcovers twitched and the light changed as he flicked the pink duvet back and away from her space.

Without a moment for thought she acted. Her finger jabbed down hard on the plastic button and she straightened her arm aiming directly at his eyes. As the spray hit him he yelled out, harsh and piercing. Shock and pain combined to send him back onto his behind. She slithered out and across the carpet. He was a huge man but temporarily incapacitated.

The sharp, but brief pain wasn't going to hold him; she knew that. He had thrown one arm out to balance while the other was across his eyes. She stamped down hard on his flexed fingers and was rewarded by another yell. The sickening crack as small bones fractured was followed by a more piercing scream. She stamped again and as the figure on the floor rolled away from the source of his agony she leaped across him and made for the door.

He was swearing now and pushing to his feet. She ran from the room, slamming the door behind her. It wouldn't hold him for long but it would give her an extra moment. Her feet flew across the landing and down the stairs. The thud of the door hitting the bedroom wall and the roar of anger told her she had moments only to unlock the bank of bolts that Pete had fastened so securely a couple of hours ago. She wouldn't make it, there was no chance. Already he was across the small space at the top of the stairs. There were bolts and chains and dead locks requiring screw keys. It was impossible.

Spinning through one hundred and eighty degrees she kept her eyes down. If she looked up and saw him then it was possible that fear would overwhelm her. The hallway was narrow and short, in moments she was in the kitchen.

At last a small piece of luck, he had left the garden door open. She was through it and turning instinctively towards the road. Pete and his captor were at the bottom of the back garden so she must go to the front and away. A tall wooden gate closed off the access and she ran at it. Grabbing out at the metal handle she dragged and pushed but it was secure. A wheelie bin stood beside the wall and she clambered onto the wobbling top. As a security breech someone's head should roll but for now it was a life saver. In just moments she'd dropped to the paved path at the side of the house. Adrenaline and muscles made strong by her outdoor life carried her forward.

The little car was yards away. He would have locked it surely? She hurried to it and snatched at the passenger door handle. Unbelievably he had left it unlocked, perhaps for just such a situation, perhaps in the rush to stop her stretching and bending as they had been visible on the pavement earlier; but for whatever reason it was open.

Leaning in she popped the little door of the glove compartment and thrust her hand to the back where she knew she would find the tiny tag of cotton. She took a deep breath as his words echoed in her mind. You'll have to do it slowly; if not it'll twist and that's a bugger.

"Slowly, slowly," she muttered under her breath, "slowly." It moved and began to slide towards her. "Slowly." As soon as there was space she pushed her hand into the dark recess and grabbed the pistol hidden there. She had no idea whether it was loaded and didn't know how to fire something she had always been afraid of. She supposed there would be a safety catch but had no idea what that was or how to release it but she grabbed at the handle and dragged the thing into the light. The gate at the side of the house began to swing backwards.

She ran back up the path, the gun heavy in her hand. She peered down at it as she hurried forward and wrapped her hand around the metal handle. Her finger curled naturally on the trigger.

He was stood before her now, cradling his damaged hand. Time stilled, there was no sound in this world where she stood, armed and facing a man whose only aim was to hurt her. The thundering in her chest and the sound of her breathing was all there was in this pivotal moment. She had killed already to protect herself; didn't they always say the second time was easier?

Chapter 42

With both arms stretched straight in front brandishing the weapon, Pauline stepped forward. The thug hadn't moved. His eyes were unsure but his stance was confrontational. He wasn't going to run, but for now just sized up the situation. Measuring the threat and weighing his options.

She moved again, another two steps. He held his injured limb across his chest but raised the other hand palm towards her. "Come on, love. You don't want to be waving that about. Just put it down. You know you don't want to hurt anyone."

"Go back, just go back. Down the garden. You have to let us go."

"Look love, you've got yourself mixed up in some nasty stuff here but we know you didn't mean to. We know you got drawn in. We won't hurt you. Give us the memory stick and whatever else you still have and that'll be that. Don't worry about Pete, that's another issue and nothing to do with you."

"I don't have it. I never had any of it."

"Yeah, so you say. Well sorry, love, but that won't wash. You just need to hand it over and you can be on your way. We don't need to have any more trouble. If you decide to be difficult, well..." He shrugged. Pauline jerked the hand holding the little gun and in response he waved his arm. "Steady now, take care with that." She was very frightened but her instinct to run was hampered by the knowledge that Pete was at the bottom of the garden and if she left him, surely he would come to harm.

She didn't know how to help him, not really. The only thing now was to go to where he was and to take him the weapon. To do the other thing, to turn and run, leaving him to his fate, was unthinkable. First though there was this other person to deal with.

She strode forward now with greater purpose. "Move down the garden." He frowned and shook his head but took a small step backwards.

The crack of a firearm discharging fractured the drowsy quiet of the suburban street.

"Christ!" The thug turned towards the source of the sound behind him, down the garden beside the shed. As he swivelled, Pauline hurled herself the last few steps and barrelled into him knocking him sideways.

Injured as he was, he tried to reach out but she scuttled past and ran to where she had last seen Pete. He was heading towards her across the grass, waving his arm, gesturing to her to turn and make for the gate but the way was barred by the other man.

Pete was beside her now and together they ran towards the gate. He reached across and grabbed the pistol, pushing her backwards so that he was between her and the gateway. Moments later the sound of a second shot rang out. The thug at the gate ducked and dived back inside the open door of the kitchen. They pushed forward, down the path and into the car. In moments they were speeding through the narrow street as the sound of police sirens grew in the distance.

"Shit, shit! Well that's it; we are now well and truly buggered!" Terror had stolen her voice and all Pauline could do was stare at him as he thumped a hand in fury against the steering wheel.

"Right. What the hell do I do now?" Surely he didn't expect any answer. She was shocked and confused, her world spinning out of control. Nothing made sense, her brain was refusing to process the information it was receiving. One hand hung on to the door handle and the other braced against the seat to steady herself as Pete threw the car around the corners, heading back to the motorway.

"Is he dead?"

"What?"

"The man at the end of the garden. Did you kill him?"

"No, no. We fought and I fired at him but I didn't hit him. Just scared him shitless."

"I'm glad."

"Yeah, so am I. You have no idea the bother it causes." He gave a short laugh.

"So, where are we going?"

"Any idea would be welcome at this point." She drew in a sharp breath and Pete glanced across the narrow space. "No, no don't worry. I'm kidding. It's fine. We need to go to another place I know. It's fine, just keep calm. Hey, you did really well back there. I don't think I would have got away if you hadn't had the gun and kept Skip busy."

"Skip?"

"Yeah, that big gorilla. Can you believe it? Skip."

By this time they had reached the slip road for the motorway and joined the stream of traffic. It felt safer to be here travelling to anywhere away from that ill-fated house and as the tumultuous day wound towards its close she found herself once again swept by the tide of fate with no option but to go with the flow.

Chapter 43

They headed north. Pauline recognised names on the road signs and the scenery became more familiar. Most of the time she sat silently, her mind reeling, thoughts scuttering back and forth. When she mentally relived the past day, it was hard to convince herself it had really happened. There had been gun fire, hulking thugs and a desperate escape. More drama heaped on the turmoil since her flight from the Dales. It was as if she had passed through a curtain into another reality yet here she was, real and whole, sitting in a warm car hurtling along the motorway.

Pete spent the first part of the drive flipping his gaze frequently to the rear view mirror. Now and then he would change lanes and tuck in between the many great trucks; after a while they would speed up again. At first this all seemed random and edgy until she realised that he was watching the traffic and allowing suspect cars from behind them to pull in front and roar away. It scared her, it quietened the obvious questions that she wanted to ask. She didn't want to draw his attention to herself and break his concentration.

Now though, nearing the Midlands, he had visibly relaxed. His shoulders drooped a little and the flick of his eyes to the mirror became more natural.

"Are we okay now?"

"Yeah. I think so. If there is anyone following us they are being very discreet and the crowd that we are dealing with don't do discreet."

"Do you know where we're going? Well, what I mean is do you have a destination in mind?"

"Yes. I'll tell you what, there's a service area up ahead. Shall we go and have a cup of coffee, a bite to eat and I'll bring you up to scratch. God, you must be so confused. I'm sorry if I've scared you. You have been amazing you know. Most people would have fallen apart or caused a fuss. I'm very impressed."

His words wrapped her in a warm glow. She was glad of the need for him to concentrate on the road because, try as she might to quell it, a grin spread across her face. It had been so long since anyone had paid her a compliment and she had forgotten how wonderful it felt to earn approval.

"Well, I haven't had a lot of choice have I." She attempted to cover her pleasure with flippancy and was rewarded by a chuckle from the other side of the car.

"I guess not. Anyway, here we are, just about half a mile to go and then we can have a chat."

The services were huge and busy. As they pushed through the rotating door they were assaulted by the smell of burgers, chips and coffee, and the noise of hundreds of travellers milling and pushing about in the brightly lit space.

"I need the ladies."

"Yeah, me too. Well, no – I mean." They began to giggle and as they made their way through the busy crowd the shared humour bound them, made them into a unit. Pauline was reminded again of how empty and lonely her life had become while she had been with George.

Unexpectedly anger welled towards her husband and his theft of so much of her life. She pushed it away for it was of no use to her now, but no matter what happened from now on she was never going to give herself away again.

They bought coffee and sandwiches and found a table in a corner near the window with a clear view of the doors. The coffee was hot and strong and as she sipped it, the last little worm of worry began to uncoil and disappear. The tall, bulky man sitting opposite to her wasn't exactly handsome, but he was imposing, with a charisma that drew glances from passing women. Pauline basked in the silly little glow of pride that came from being with a man whom other women admired. If only. The thought brought with it a sweep of sadness because of course this wasn't real, none of it was based on truth and tears sprung into her eyes with the knowledge that it wouldn't last. This precious experience would be swept away with the return of normality. She sighed and he leaned towards her, stretching out a hand to touch hers where it curled around the warm cup.

"Are you okay?"

She nodded and dredged up a smile. "I'm fine." Pete nodded and looked down at the table for a moment. He collected his thoughts and then looked back at her. His eyes were serious but clear and honest and she steeled herself for what was to come.

"Well, put simply, I think we are safe at the moment. I don't know what happened back at the house, though it does prove that there is a leak somewhere in the group I'm working with. I find that hard to accept but there can't be any doubt now. It means that we have to look out for ourselves. I am heading for a place that is just mine. It's nothing to do with the job and nobody I work with knows about it. I'm not supposed to have it but…" He shrugged and grinned at her. "Is that okay?"

"Erm, well yes. I don't really know what you mean… but… what choice do I have?"

"Well, you could go to the police. I could take you. I should do that really; I should hand you over and sort it all out officially, but right now I don't know whom to trust and I'm not very happy to put myself in a position where I'm not in charge."

"But if we go to your place then what?"

"Good question. I just want to get us safe. Once I have done that I can try and find out whom to trust and what the situation is regarding the gang."

"Pete?"

"Yes."

"Have you got the diamonds and the memory stick?"

"Yes. I have. The diamonds are not that important but the memory stick is priceless. The information on there could lead to the arrest of a huge gang of people traffickers. It's taken me a couple of years to get it. I have to be very careful with it. Because of the problems with the unit I can't hand it over; I have to handle it myself. It's complicated and really, though it seems hard to say this, it doesn't actually concern you. Not that side of it; what has happened since the road accident is another issue and we have to sort that out as well."

"Where is the body, the one from the cliffs?"

"It's gone. It's in the ocean." Pauline's hand flew to her mouth. "That is something else that we have to deal with. You could just walk away from it, Pauline. I know you did what you did because you were in danger. You could just take back your life and carry on."

She shook her head. "How can I do that? How can I live with that? Is it right that I should?"

"Well, what are your other options? The police in Cornwall searched, they didn't find a body."

"But we ran away. Won't they think that was odd?"

"I've been in touch. I had to make sure they kept an eye on your friends at the farm. I told them you were helping us and they were only too happy to wash their hands of it all. Right now the file there is closed, marked for no further action. You can just walk away from it.

"The trouble is the people who came to the house are aware of you. They think that you have the memory stick. So until I sort that out I can't promise you that you are safe. Will you trust me for just a while longer? Will you come with me and let me try to make it all right?"

"Yes."

Chapter 44

By the time they pulled off the motorway onto minor roads, the day was fading. Yellow lights from the windows of roadside houses pooled on pavements and verges and commuter vehicles mustered on overcrowded drives. The world settled into evening.

Pauline didn't recognise the area. They drove through a small town. A carbon copy of so many others. The main road carving the centre into north and south was lined with ubiquitous retail outlets and fast food restaurants: it was Everywhere and Nowhere.

Out at the other side of the built-up areas gentle hills rose away on either side. The illumination from an occasional grand home or farmhouse shone out, oases in the deepening darkness. It was peaceful and calm in the warm car with Pete beside her and Pauline felt that if they drove on forever in this half dream state she would have been happy to accept the endless journey as her fate.

After another hour, when they were far out in the country, he turned off the road and bumbled down a rutted track. Trees lined either side of the narrow lane with the occasional gateway the only evidence of intermittent human activity. He pulled into one of the openings, and turned off the lights. The engine was the only sound gently thrumming into the stillness of a late summer night.

"Is this where we're staying?"

"No, no of course not. I just want to make sure we're on our own." The flash of his grin in the dark interior soothed her nerves. This was what he did; he was calm, in charge and everything was under control. Pauline settled back into the seat and closed her eyes. She felt safe.

When Pete was happy that no-one had followed they drew back out and travelled the last mile down the country road. He climbed from the car and pushed open a wooden gate.

"Pass me that torch will you." Pauline passed him the heavy flashlight from the parcel shelf and he left her in the darkness. As he made his way down the short drive the cone of light swung back and forth through the tiny garden towards the darker shadow of a building hunkered down amongst the trees.

She could see him in the distance as he walked down a side passage. Then for a while she was in almost total darkness as he checked around the back, emerging at the other side, and at last joining her back in the car.

"Okay. It looks good. Welcome to my place." He smiled at her across the narrow space and her heart flipped and she acknowledged at last what she already knew deep inside. She was attracted to him, this man about whom she knew nothing and who she had met in the most horrible of circumstances. She was drawn to him and his nearness in the darkness excited her.

The thought of going into a strange house with him now, alone, caused a thrill that had been, until now, a memory of other days.

He took the car around the back of the building and parked it hidden among overgrown bushes. The path to the little door was gravel winding between what was probably a rough lawn. Here and there a shrub hunched, darker grey than the ambient dimness, but the scent was of wildness rather than roses. It was wonderful.

The great key he pulled from his pocket slid smoothly into the lock and in moments they stepped onto the flagged floor of a large space. Pauline waited quietly in the doorway as Pete moved with the ease of long familiarity into the house. The click of a lighter and flicker of a tiny flame grew into a golden glow as he lit the wick of an old hurricane lamp which sat on a heavy wooden table.

"Don't panic," he muttered. "We have electric, but it's only left on in the utility room, there are isolator switches, I have to turn it on for the rest of the place, and anyway I kinda like this in the kitchen. Come in, sit down."

She walked across the hard stone. "I like the lantern as well. But I don't need to sit down, Pete. It's nice to stretch my legs." She took another step towards him. He held his ground. She lifted a hand and placed it gently, questioningly on his upper arm. His head bent towards her, just a little. She lifted her face to his and as their lips met she felt as though she had reached her safe haven. His arms wrapped around her, firm and strong and comforting and as their bodies touched chest and hips, the warmth grew.

It felt right and good and honest and she knew she would be his, if he wanted it.

Chapter 45

"I can't. We shouldn't. Pauline, I don't think this is a good idea."

"I know." She smiled at him and his lips lifted as he pulled back his head and looked down at her.

"It's wrong in so many ways."

"I know." She lifted a hand to his face and laid it across his cheek. Her head tipped to one side and her eyes searched his, seeking the truth of what he wanted.

For a while they stood arms around each other in the slightly damp kitchen. Outside an owl called and in the quiet house the little lantern hissed and fizzed.

"Pauline…" His voice was hoarse and doubt flashed across his face and still she didn't move but simply stood in the shelter of his arm, waiting. "Are you sure?" He read her stillness for what it was. She nodded.

"I haven't been here for a while. The beds might need airing." The everyday tone of the comment drew a giggle from her.

"Right." She smiled and took his hand.

He lifted the lantern and they walked into the gloom of the hallway. Stepping in front he drew her after him, down the narrow space and up the stairs.

The landing was a small square. In the flickering light she saw a bathroom, the door ajar and the porcelain gleaming whitely in the gloom. There were three other rooms, he pushed the door of the nearest.

He turned to her again. "Okay?"

She slipped in front of him and stepped inside the space. The bed was made up. The curtains were open and the glow of moonlight glinted on a mirror and shone on polished wood. It was chilly, with the feel of a room just wakening from the torpor of neglect and emptiness.

She walked to the bed and threw back the covers running a hand over the sheet. "It's fine. Cold, but not damp."

He was close behind her now and his arms snaked around her waist drawing her back against him. "Are you sure about this?"

His concern threw her. She had never experienced such consideration before. For a moment she wondered if he was trying to draw away kindly, back off without hurting her. She twisted around until she could look him in the eye. There was nothing there but kindness.

"I like you Pete. I'm happy here in this moment."

He nodded.

His fingers found the buttons on her blouse. As he twisted the tiny pieces of plastic she closed her eyes to savour the illicit pleasure that had come so unexpectedly. As he pulled the fabric from her shoulders she felt a frisson of fear. What would he think of her? She was no longer a girl. She had stayed slim, kept herself fit, but her breasts and her stomach were those of a forty-year old. He lowered his head and his lips played across her shoulders. She felt the flutter of his kisses on her neck and then her breath was taken as he raised a hand to her breast, to hold and to gently tease.

She pulled at his shirt and the belt of his jeans. When they were unfastened and in a heap at his feet he stepped out of them and with a grin he pulled off his socks.

Pauline slipped out of her trousers and climbed onto the bed dragging the chilly duvet over her. He pulled it aside to snuggle underneath and then wrapped her to him and held her in his warm arms. Their legs twined and their breath mingled and she found with him a kindness, a generosity and a pleasure that she had never known before.

Chapter 46

Unfamiliar greys and shadows disoriented her and the bulk of a body in the bed was strange and unsettling in her half-waking state. Pauline lay still and quiet until dream and reality divided and she remembered it all. Where and who and why. Pete murmured and turning, drew her into the warmth of his sleeping body. As she curled into him tears came to her eyes for she knew that this could not be and it broke her heart to have what she couldn't hold.

She didn't sleep again. The curtains were open and dawn unveiled a new day and the rustle of leaves and patter of rain on the window spoke of dying summer. She pressed closer to the man beside her and revelled in the comfort and what she knew was to be a fleeting happiness.

Pete woke and smiled across the rumpled pillows and kissed her face and neck and they made love slowly. His hands caressed the rounds and hollows of her body. As they stroked and teased and nibbled she lost herself in his gentleness and generosity and finally in the urgency of their mutual need. She had never known it could be like this...

Later she slid from the bed and dragged on Pete's discarded T-shirt. She pulled it down to cover her behind and then laughed as he raised his eyebrows at the coyness after their recent familiarity. She felt sated and soothed by their intimacy and more than that, he had made her feel whole, and even more yet she felt beautiful and womanly.

She didn't want to spoil the moment but knew life would go on and they must leave this room and this moment.

"Can I have a shower?"

"Did I do the electric thing last night?"

"I don't know. I don't think so."

"Right. Give me a minute and I'll sort it. God, I'm starving."

His legs swung from the bed and he leaned to retrieve his boxers from the tangle of clothes on the floor. She watched and felt emotion flood her body. She could love this man.

His voice came from downstairs in the hallway. "Okay Pauline, the heat's on. I'm going to fish in the freezer and get breakfast underway."

"Thanks." The bathroom was spotless and it was obvious that, though the house had been unlived in, someone kept it clean. The airing cupboard held a pile of towels and there was shampoo. She paused at the sight of the bottle on the glass shelf. Shampoo.

It wasn't her business. She picked up the bottle and realised with a tiny thud of disappointment that it was open and partly used. So, someone else came here and used the bathroom and cleaned and polished. It wasn't her business.

The smell of bacon and coffee made her mouth water. With a hint of distaste she pulled on yesterday's underwear and blouse. Her fingers hovered over the handle of a drawer but in the end it was too much of an invasion of privacy to pull it forward. In truth she didn't want to see. If there was underwear in there, women's underwear, she couldn't borrow it anyway and the bright, loving morning would be besmirched. Shampoo? Well shampoo could just be a cheap shower gel or perhaps he sometimes let his hair grow and so would need it, but underwear, women's clothes... There would be no denying the meaning of those.

The kitchen was bright and the pine table held plates of bacon sandwiches. Coffee dripped into a pitcher on the machine beside the sink. It was homely and cosy. Pauline was starving, because of course they had eaten very little yesterday. She fell on the food with an enthusiasm that brought a smile to Pete's face.

"How come you have all this?"

"I keep bread, bacon and so on in the freezer, out in the utility room. I never know when I'm going to come here and so I try to keep it stocked."

"Is this your house then? Your own... not a police house or something?"

"Yes, this is mine. I bought it a few years ago. I needed to know that no matter what, I had a place that was wholly mine and was safe. I needed a home."

"It's lovely."

"Thanks. I have someone come in to keep an eye on things. Marie, from the farm back the way we came in. She thinks I work abroad. It's safer for her that way."

"It's dangerous isn't it? Your job, what you do?"

"Sometimes it is. Sometimes it's boring and tedious."

"How long have you been doing it?"

He leaned across the space between them and laid his hand on hers. "Pauline. I think it's best, for now at least, if you don't know too much about what's going on. Too much about me."

There it was, the barrier. His life, the things that he did. His past and his future; she wasn't to be a real part of any of it and now the sandwich stuck in her throat as her heart filled with sadness and reality hit her in the gut.

Chapter 47

He had gone. "Don't worry, you're safe here. Don't go out though. It's best if you stay in for now."

With Pete's final word of warning ringing in her ears she had stood by the window and watched as he drove back down the little lane.

Before he left, he had offered to pick up some essentials while he was out. "I'll be a couple of hours but on the way back I can go to town." It had been a strange conversation and the memory brought a grin to her face. He stood before her indicating with a sweep of his hand down the length of her body. "What erm, size are you? You know… for underwear and… well I don't really know what you'd buy."

"I take size twelve knickers, anything will do, not a thong though."

"Knickers, right." He lowered his eyes to hide the laughter, but she saw his shoulders quake and rescued him with a giggle.

"Don't worry about a bra, I can manage if you don't mind me washing it through tonight."

"Shall I look for a T-shirt?"

"Oh, would you? Yes, please. A T-shirt and something to sleep in would be great. The knickers, and perhaps some conditioner. My hair feels like straw after the beach."

"You look fine to me." He had grinned widely at her then and held out a hand. She walked to him and leaned into his hug. While her face was buried in his chest he had spoken quietly. "Are you okay with what happened? I mean, you know, you don't regret it?"

"No, no I don't. It was lovely. I like you a lot, Pete." She lifted her eyes and a glimpse of something in his expression had stopped her there. She knew. Deep down she knew that there was no future for them. He knew it too, didn't he? Well, didn't he?

After he had gone she cleaned the kitchen counters and tidied the breakfast things away. Another cup of coffee was just a way to pass the time and in the end half of it was poured down the drain.

For a while she sat and looked through the magazines she found on the coffee table in the living room. They didn't reveal anything about him. They were out of date news magazines and one or two that looked as though they might have been picked up in airports. There was nothing in them to hold her interest.

The book cases were well stocked and she pulled down a novel. She curled up on the sofa and tried to lose herself in the story but even that couldn't hold her attention. She was on edge and fidgety.

The sun teased her through the narrow window, birds called and white puffs floated across the clean blue sky. It was too nice a day to be inside.

She walked back into the kitchen and stood at the open door. There was no-one around. Cows in a distant field lowed now and again. The lazy smoke from a fire somewhere to the north smudged the horizon. She stepped into the patch of back garden. Sparrows and dunnocks hopped around the base of a hawthorn hedge.

Tufty grass covered most of the space with just one small apple tree in the corner. A couple of pots held geraniums. Marie from the farm had obviously kept an eye on the bright little plants which flanked a wooden bench. It tempted her, the old wood worn to comfort.

Two steps from the house, that wasn't out was it, surely? She crossed the narrow flagstones and lowered herself to the seat. The sun warmed her face and painted bright colours on the back of her closed lids as she gave herself to the peace. There was time enough for worry and maybe even regret later. At this moment she would just be…

Her shoulders slumped as drowsiness fell like a silk curtain and her mind began to drift. She should pull back, get up and move around, but the harmony had her, the air and the music of the earth was carrying her away and it was just too hard to come back. Maybe just another few minutes and then she would force herself awake.

She didn't hear the car, or the footsteps in the meadow. She didn't feel the shadow cool her skin and when the terror hit her it came from out of a place of gentle peace and was all the more brutal for that.

Chapter 48

The bliss of sun and birdsong was, in an instant, a nightmare. There was pain in her cheeks and the world spun and tipped as the bench tumbled backwards. She was restricted, held, choking. Her head shook desperately from side to side.

She had to get it off. Whatever had her, she had to shake it loose.

In seconds the true horror hit her. She was gripped from behind. A hand across her face, over her mouth, squeezing the flesh and skin of her cheeks tightly, sparking water to her eyes. She flailed with her arms, kicked out with her legs but he pulled her sideways and backwards, away from the upended seat. She kicked over a pot of geraniums. Still he had her. She writhed and bucked and tried to scream. But he had her and was dragging her back into the house.

"Don't go out," Pete had said. He was going to be so angry. She was crying, snot running from her nose.

"Shit. That's gross." She was thrown to the floor. Her chin hit the hard flagstones and stars whirled in a world of grey, and when her vision cleared she saw blood, spattered across the grey paving. She turned her head but he was sitting on her now. The weight of him would surely break her spine. She was trapped and terrified. The scream that issued from her throat came from a distance, unreal.

Her was hair dragged upwards and then a hand swiped across her mouth. Panic took her to yet another level of desperation. She couldn't breathe now; he had taped her lips. He leaned down close to her ear. As he did the weight of him eased a little but still she couldn't draw breath into her lungs.

"Quiet now. Breathe through your nose. Breathe through your nose. Slowly." It was almost gentle, a whisper in her ear. She could feel the disturbance of air on her neck. "That's better. Slowly, in through your nose. You'll be okay if you do that. Worst thing you can do is panic. You panic and you'll likely choke."

She dragged tiny breaths in through her nostrils, little snorts.

He dragged her hands backwards and she felt the tape wrapped around her wrists. She squealed anew, consumed by anger, frustration and fear.

"Quiet. Lie still. He rolled away and there was a grunt as he pushed to his feet beside her.

Grabbing her legs, he taped her ankles and then pulled her upright. A chair scraped across the floor and with a painful grip on her shoulders he pushed her onto the seat.

"Right. We are going to wait here. We are going to be quiet. We are not going to have any trouble. Do you understand me?" Again, the searing pain as her head was pulled backwards. "I said do you understand me?" She tried to nod but he still held her hair.

"You are going to sit still in that chair. I am going to be right here and we are just going to wait." She tried now to turn her head and the blow from his fist brought back the swirl of dizziness. "Don't. Don't even think about it."

Long moments of silence followed and, though it was still uncomfortable, she gained control of her breathing. It was like the cave all over again. He was dead though, the man in the cave. Pete had told her he was gone, tossed in the sea. So, she had escaped that horror to find herself yet again tied and gagged and beaten. It was all too much.

She had taken all she could. She wanted to just drift away. She was finished. It seemed that there was to be no way out of this drama and it was all too hard. The sobbing made breathing impossible again. Tears tickled her cheeks and as phlegm gathered in her throat she felt the panic returning. Like a dog she shook her head and was rewarded with another drag on her hair.

"Quiet! For God's sake, bitch, be quiet! You're not doing yourself any favours here and you causing us trouble is just going to make things worse. Now keep still." He moved behind and his feet slapped on the kitchen flags. Another chair was dragged to where she was, just behind her and facing the door.

She remembered a poem, something from long ago. Something about a highwayman and a woman watching and waiting with no way of warning her lover but to die.

Pete had surely been her lover but for him she couldn't even find a way to die.

Chapter 49

She heard a car. The low rumble grew and was joined by the spit of gravel under tyres. Next there was the whisper of grass as Pete drove to the hiding place among shrubs at the rear of the house.

The thug sitting behind her tensed and chair legs scraped across the floor. Pauline's heart pounded, the pulse in her ears was near to pain. She shook her head back and forth and stamped her bound feet up and down. Anything that she could think of to make a row, to warn him. She was rewarded for the effort by a hard blow against the side of her head that sent her senses reeling again. The iron taste of warm blood and the liquid gathering in her throat told of more damage to the delicate lining of her mouth. Still she rocked back and forth, the wooden chair rattling in the quiet.

Would he hear? If he did would he understand, and even then what could he do? He mustn't come through the door. Now at last she had a glimpse of her attacker. The dark figure stepped forward. He was dressed in black with a hooded top. The fabric was pulled forward and down so that there was no way to see his face from where she was. Dark leather gloves covered his hands. As he moved forward he kicked out at her. "Quiet, bitch!" It was an aside, almost nonchalant. His voice was lowered now to a hiss.

Tears blinded her. She couldn't let this happen. The monster waiting to blast Pete out of existence was calm, his hands steady as he raised the gun and aimed at the door. Again, she rattled the chair. Now she tried to stand, shuffling forward and then pushing herself up using the strength in her thigh muscles. As she slid from the seat and straightened her legs he turned to her, lowering his hands and giving her a glimpse of the lethal weapon held before him. The bottom of his face was hidden behind a scarf or deep collar, all that was visible were his eyes peering at her.

He raised the gun again and pointed it directly at her face. Her bladder failed her now as buzzing filled her ears. She thought that she would faint and in truth would welcome the oblivion but footfalls on the flagstones held her in the moment.

Desperate squeals from deep in her throat were of no use as a warning. She let her legs collapse, dropping herself back down to the chair, intent on knocking it to the floor. Her only thought now was to make as much noise as possible in her weak and hobbled state. Misjudging the distance between herself and the seat she toppled backwards and in the event accomplished her aim by accident. As the chair tipped she tumbled onto it and landed hard on the upended legs which poked agonisingly into her stomach. The pain was indescribable but the noise was satisfying.

Now the gunman swung his weapon down and she twisted her head to look into the evil of his eyes and believed that the moment of her death was upon her.

The rattle of the door handle had him swinging back, caught between the need for revenge and the execution of his plan. Pauline took the momentary diversion to roll from the broken frame of the chair and try to tuck herself under the table. She drew up her legs, intent on making herself as small as possible and protecting the most vulnerable areas of her body. She was sobbing and choking in a world of fear and hurt.

The intruder swung his head around and glared one more time before straightening. "I'll save you for later, bitch, and you'll regret what you just did."

Now he turned back to the door, took a step, another, and then raised the gun.

Pauline screwed her eyes shut. It was over. There was nothing she could do. Pete would open the door of his haven and be shot before he even registered that there was a problem. She couldn't bear it.

The click of the door lock filled the quiet of the summer afternoon. A pale dagger of sunlight speared across the grey flagstone floor. Dust motes disturbed by the sudden breeze danced and twinkled merrily and then the air was riven by the shock of the gunshot echoing through the old house and sending screaming birds spiralling into the cloud freckled sky.

Chapter 50

Pete was calling to her in the darkness. Pauline needed to go to him, to help him. She had to find him and make him whole again.

The pain in head and stomach held her back. Though her heart tried to drive her forward, her body was broken. She had to move. Something held her down. Strong arms restricted movement. She heard him calling and if she didn't find him he would die.

She didn't want him to die.

She didn't want to die.

* * *

"Pauline, Pauline, lie still. It's okay, you're okay. Just try to relax. We need to take care of you."

Now the light came, floating before her eyes, swooping and receding. "I hurt."

"You're alright, Pauline. We're going to take care of you. Just relax."

The small, sharp pain in her arm became a soothing caress, sweeping through the discomfort and befuddling her mind. Nothing mattered now. She could drift away and it would all be over and she could find Pete.

"Pete?" She felt her lips move and the sound was close. Had she spoken?

"It's okay, Pauline. I'm here with you. It's all fine. We're okay."

Against the weight of medication, she forced open her eyelids and his face floated above hers. He smiled at her. She had found him.

Now she let the darkness sweep her away...

* * *

Even before she opened her eyes the sounds, smells and sensations told her where she was. She had been in a hospital before.

Her throat was dry. There was a dull ache at the back of her eyes so she stayed in the dark for a while longer. The whirl of dreams and confusion cleared slowly and nibbles of memory flicked in and out of her consciousness. Then it was time; she knew she must open her eyes and face reality.

He was sitting in a chair beside the bed. Though he had a magazine in his hand, his eyes flicked often towards where she was lying. Finally, they made contact and he gave her a smile.

"Hi there."

"Pete." The sound was little more than a croak. He leaned towards her and took the plastic beaker from the bedside table. He helped her to drink.

"I thought you were dead. I thought he shot you."

"I know, you made that clear when we were trying to help you. You were pretty upset."

"What happened? Why am I here?"

"Okay, second question first I think. You hurt your stomach. You ruptured your spleen. It looked as though you fell on the chair leg. They don't think you need to have an operation but it's going to be sore for a while."

"I tried to knock it over, the chair. I tried to make a noise. Did you hear?"

"I did, but I already knew that something was wrong. That brings us to the first question I suppose. I saw the bench and the plants."

"Oh of course, I forgot about them. I broke the pot. I'm sorry."

"Don't be, that's what gave the game away. If it hadn't been for that I would have walked straight in and… well I guess we might not be having this conversation now."

"Is he…?"

"He's dead. He can't hurt you anymore."

"Oh Pete, your lovely home. I'm so sorry." Now the tears began and he pulled a tissue from the box on her locker. "It's all spoiled for you now. Your peaceful place. It's all my fault."

She was sobbing and he pressed the buzzer to call for a nurse. They had said that he mustn't upset her and he was helpless in the face of her distress.

"Don't be silly. It's not your fault, what on earth do you mean?"

"If you hadn't taken me there. It's all my fault. Everything."

He moved closer and reached down. He took her hand. "No, how can you say that, it's ridiculous."

"But if I hadn't interfered, right at the start. Back in the Dales, if I hadn't gone into the ditch and got involved."

"No, no. You couldn't help it. What else could you have done? Don't be silly, Pauline."

A young nurse slid quietly into the room. "Hi there, Pauline, I'm Carol. You need to try and keep calm. Doctor Miller will be along later and he won't be very happy with me if he finds you all upset.

"I'm going to give you something to help you to calm down. Is that okay."

She didn't wait for an answer but added drugs to the infusion, checked the monitor readings and then offered a fleeting smile towards Pete, "You can have five more minutes and then I think Pauline should have a rest, okay?"

He nodded. "It's all fine, Pauline. We've sorted it all. The job's over. It wasn't quite as successful as we had hoped but we saved some women from hell. We can probably put some really bad guys behind bars and, hey, I'm still here."

She felt herself begin to drift. "Will you come back?"

"Yes, of course. Someone will need to talk to you about what happened anyway. Nothing to worry about, but just to keep things in order. I'll see you in the morning. Sleep now." His lips brushed her forehead as she fell into a deep warm pit.

She was safe, he was safe. All was well.

Chapter 51

"Are you sure about this, Pauline." The concern in Pete's eyes made her heart contract with affection.

"I am. It's fine."

The Dales were glorious in early autumn. A great sweep of sky brushed the horizon and high in the blue was the dark pinprick of a merlin or maybe even the precious falcon. It was magical and it was still home.

The agent in France had assured her that all was in order and the work on her holiday homes could begin in her absence and *"Madam must not worry but must get well soon from her accident."* It had been too complicated to explain and so a vague story of a fall had sufficed.

"Go over the top will you, Pete."

"That'll take us past the place where the accident happened."

"Yes, that's the point. I want to lay the ghost. It's just a road and a ditch."

"You astound me, you really do. You are so sensible and grounded. You're tough as well. The doctors said at least ten days in hospital and it's barely a week."

"Well, it's true what they say, though it's a cliché and all. The things that didn't kill me – well I don't know that they made me stronger but they certainly made me realise that I can cope with stuff."

"Bloody hell you certainly can. Does he know you're coming today?"

"George? Yes, I called him to confirm yesterday."

"Are you still sure you don't want me to come in with you? If he was to hurt you after all you've been through…" Pete lifted a hand from the wheel and reached to squeeze hers where it lay in her lap.

"Oh, he won't. One thing that has never been surer is that. He will never hurt me again."

They drove in silence for a while. Though she had insisted on her release from the hospital, Pauline still felt fragile. The pain of careless movement would cause her to draw in a sharp breath.

"Afterwards, will you call me?"

"I will. Don't worry. I'm okay now and I have to do this. Everything that went wrong, it all happened because I wasn't doing this right."

"Oh, that's just mumbo jumbo. It would have happened no matter what. You did what you had to do and the rest of it was out of your hands."

"I believe it was because what I was doing was wrong. I shouldn't have been sneaking away like that."

"I'm worried about you."

She smiled at his words. "That's nice, Pete, but, you know, I think that all the bad things that could happen to me have happened now, eh."

"God, I hope so. Listen, I've got my phone. Any problems, any hint of a problem, call me and I'll be there."

"I know, I know you will." She pointed now out of the window to the place just ahead of them. He slowed the car.

"Look, there's the ditch, the corner. See I told you, it's just a road and a bend."

She smiled at him, but inside her heart leaped and her stomach coiled. Here was the start of it all. She made a sudden decision. "Stop, stop here. I'll get out. I'll walk from here."

"Here? No, you can't. Bloody hell, Pauline! How much do you want to put yourself through?"

"I'll walk from here, Pete."

"You amaze me, you really do."

"Oh, go on. You, with what you do! But thank you; it's nice to hear.

"Kiss me." He drew into the side of the country road, bare yards from the scene of the accident.

A dark stain still bore witness to the sacrificed sheep. He turned off the engine. He leaned and drew her into his arms and kissed her deep and long and then drew back to gaze into her eyes.

"You truly do amaze me." The only response she could give was a smile, for her heart was full and emotion choked her.

"I know we can't be together, Pete. Not really. Not in the normal way. But we can make it work, can't we?"

"I believe that you could make anything work, if you have decided to. Call me."

"I will." She stepped from the car and blew a kiss through the window as he drove past. She strode on in the reverse direction to that she had come only short weeks before.

The garden was already a little overgrown and the windows needed cleaning. She sighed, looking around at the early neglect. How sad it all was, how very sad.

She would not ring the bell. George was not going to open the door to her standing on the step like a naughty child. She had her key and as the door swung inwards he was standing in the hall. It amused her that he was dressed formally, his shirt roughly ironed but his silk tie knotted precisely. The sight of him painted a smile on her lips despite all that had happened.

"Hello Pauline."

"George."

"Come in. I was in the lounge. I've made tea." As she passed through the hall she glanced into the messy kitchen. The thought of the work that would be needed to restore it to its former pristine state lowered her mood and she sighed.

George had already thrown himself onto the settee and he turned as she stepped through the door.

"I'm glad you're back. I was worried and then the call from the hospital upset me. They wouldn't tell me much, just that you had been involved in an incident."

"No, I asked them not to tell you too much. I just wanted to come back myself without too much fuss."

"Yes, of course you did. I'm glad. Glad that you're here. Look… I know we've got some issues, Pauline. Things to work out. I'm willing to give it a go. I owe you that at least. I'll even go to counselling, if that's what you want. I can't promise to change completely, but yes, we should both make an effort. It'll be good to get back to normal. Now you're back we can settle down again."

She gazed at her husband. Looked at his dark hair shining in the afternoon light, his figure still trim and his good looks barely touched by the years. Her heart saw the young man she had married, the dashing groom standing beside the flower-decked altar.

Her eyes were drawn to his hands, resting now on his lap. When they met she had loved his hands. Manly hands, strong and sure. Hands that had held hers and slipped the ring onto her finger.

She remembered them curled into fists flying at her in fury or slapping at her in anger and she leaned towards him and wrapped her arms around the grey cushion curled on the sofa.

She gathered up the sleepy feline and without a backward glance she walked from the room. Pausing in the hall to stow Samson in his carrier, she strode on and out and into the sunshine.

Carefully she climbed into her car. She'd done it. She'd left George. Honestly and openly with her head high and back stiffened with resolve.

She'd taken the cat.

The End

If you enjoyed this book, please let others know by leaving a quick review on Amazon. Also, if you spot anything untoward in the paperback, get in touch. We strive for the best quality and appreciate reader feedback.

editor@thebookfolks.com

www.thebookfolks.com

Other books by Diane Dickson:

BROKEN ANGEL
BONE BABY
TWIST OF TRUTH
TANGLED TRUTH
WHO FOLLOWS
THE GRAVE
PICTURES OF YOU
LAYERS OF LIES
DEPTHS OF DECEPTION
YOU'RE DEAD
SINGLE TO EDINBURGH

BROKEN
ANGEL

A thrilling murder mystery, full of nail-biting suspense

Diane M. Dickson

An eerie corpse dressed as a bride, a killer playing a macabre game, and a woman detective prepared to follow her instincts. Enter DI Tanya Miller, the missing persons specialist brought in to investigate the disappearance of a woman from a motorway services. Someone is playing a sick game, and she's determined to catch him, no matter what it takes.

Available on Kindle and in paperback from Amazon.

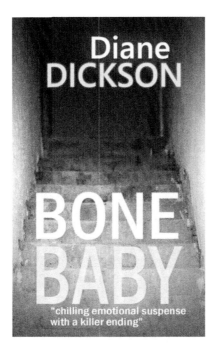

When Lily's partner dies, she is left with the burden of a dark secret that they had shared. This becomes an obsession. When Lily has the chance to right this past wrong, it sets off a chain of events that quickly spiral out of her control. Will she do the unthinkable to make things right?

Available on Kindle and in paperback from Amazon.

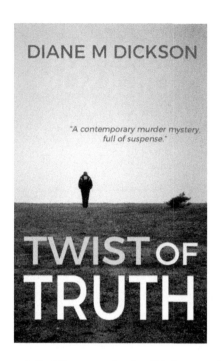

DIANE M DICKSON

"A contemporary murder mystery, full of suspense."

TWIST OF TRUTH

Having been jailed for a murder he didn't commit, Simon Fulton returns to his quiet hometown with one thing on his mind: revenge! But when he starts to enact it, he realises he has the wrong target. And the consequences of his mistake will be terrifying.

Available on Kindle and in paperback from Amazon.

"A gripping private investigator murder mystery"

TANGLED
TRUTH

Having cleared his name, Simon is deciding on how to rebuild his life. He is visited by a man who believes a family member has been wrongly convicted for a road accident that killed a girl. So begins Simon's first real private investigation, one that takes him into a tangled web of lies.

Available on Kindle and in paperback from Amazon.

Printed in Great Britain
by Amazon

26158555R00118